THE BOSS'S DAUGHTER

SAMANTHA HICKS

THE BOSS'S DAUGHTER

SAMANTHA HICKS

Affinity
Rainbow Publications

2021

The Boss's Daughter
© 2021 by Samantha Hicks

Affinity E-Book Press NZ LTD
Canterbury, New Zealand

1st Edition

ISBN: 978-1-99-004901-9

All rights reserved.

This is a work of fiction. Names, character, places, and incidents are the product of the author's imagination or are used fictitiously and any resemblance to actual persons living or dead, businesses, companies, events, or locales is entirely coincidental

Editor: CK King
Proof Editor: Alexis Smith
Cover Design: Irish Dragon Design
Production Design: Affinity Publication Services

ACKNOWLEDGMENTS

As always, the team at Affinity have done an amazing job in making my writing shine. I love working with them and hope to have many more releases with them. I appreciate all their hard work in making this book what it is today. A novel is so much more than just my words on the page. Cover design, editing, and beta reading are the elements that turn my stories into a finished product and I couldn't imagine doing it without their expertise.

I also want to thank my friends and family for supporting me in my dream of being an author and for all the little things they do for me.

And of course special mention goes to my best bud Finley. Although he can be a handful at times, I can't imagine not having him in my life. He truly is the best dog in the world.

DEDICATION

To my wonderful mother, Pamela, who has always supported me.
You're not just my mum, you're also my best friend.

TABLE OF CONTENTS

PROLOGUE

Vivian Westfall sipped her Riesling as she glanced around the company's conference hall, trying to find something to gain her attention away from Sarah and Bonnie. The two members of the sales department stood next to her, gossiping about the latest news in their division. Vivian was Chief Financial Officer of Bridger Holdings, a company that bought and sold commercial properties around the globe. After four years in the job, she still found the work interesting. Though the people Gregory Bridger employed left a lot to be desired. One thing Vivian couldn't stand was idle gossip.

"Can you believe that, Viv?" Sarah lightly touched Vivian's forearm.

"Hmm?" Vivian looked back at Sarah, her brain trying to fill in what had been said while she was busy daydreaming of getting home and soaking in a hot bath.

Sarah frowned at her. "I said, can you believe Marcus from the sales team is gay?"

Vivian blinked at the duo, not sure how to respond. Was it so unusual to work with someone who was gay these days? *I guess they don't know about my own preferences.* Vivian smiled internally. She wasn't closeted, but the need to come out at work had never arisen. She was, by nature, a very private person. She didn't think anyone even knew if she had any siblings. "Is that a problem?" She hoped she wouldn't have to deal with homophobes this early on in the evening. Bridger Holdings were having their annual spring party. Gregory liked to celebrate the end of the fiscal year by throwing an elegant bash, one that every employee was mandated to attend. Vivian knew it was his way of showing off how successful he was. In the time she had been working at Bridger, the company always turned a huge profit. She couldn't fault Gregory for being pleased with himself. He might be conceited, but he knew how to run a business.

"Um, no," Sarah said, her brows pinching ever so slightly. "It's just that he's so hot."

"Hot people can't be gay?" Jesus. Some people are so uninformed.

"Of course they can," Bonnie chimed in. "Sarah's just annoyed, because she asked him out and he shot her down."

"You don't have to tell the world, Bon." Sarah's cheeks flamed.

Vivian had to bite her lip to stop her laugh bubbling out. Apparently, it was okay to gossip about other people, but not to have the gossip be about her. "His loss." Vivian shrugged, doing her best to appear sincere. She really couldn't wait to get out of there.

A commotion over the other side of the hall grabbed her attention. She gazed across the dance floor to the makeshift bar set up along the far wall. Vivian had never seen the tall, lean blonde before. The woman was gyrating next to a horrified looking Patricia, the wife of one of the company's biggest clients. The dancing woman held a drink high above her head, sloshing the contents everywhere, some of it hitting herself.

"Oh, Christ," Bonnie whispered.

Vivian glanced at her. "Who is that?"

"You don't know?"

Vivian frowned, shaking her head.

"That's Lauren Bridger. The boss's daughter."

Vivian looked back over at Lauren, who was now gesturing wildly to the bartender. Of course, Vivian knew Gregory had a daughter but didn't expect her to be the drunk idiot across the room. Lauren was a world away from the pretty eight-year-old girl Vivian had seen in the picture frame on Gregory's desk. In the four years she had been there, she was yet to meet Lauren. Last she heard from office gossip, Lauren was off travelling the world on Gregory's money. She didn't imagine that his daughter would be so obviously drunk and making a fool of herself in front of her father's employees and important clients.

"Christ," Bonnie repeated. "The local MP is here. If he sees Lauren acting like that, he'll for sure pull his support of Gregory."

Vivian glanced over to where Bonnie pointed, spotting Adam Marshall in a small group of people. Bonnie was right. Gregory had extolled his own success plenty of times, with the story of how much he had done for the community. He had wanted to reinvest into the place he grew up in and keep his business local. Not many people had liked seeing a high-rise built in the centre of a seaside town, but Gregory had convinced the council to allow him building permission. He'd promised to donate funds to local causes and to employ as many local people as possible. He had kept that promise over the last thirty years. Adam Marshall had become a close friend of his. Seeing Lauren act this way would surely cause friction between them.

"Excuse me." Vivian handed her drink to Sarah and strode across the empty dance floor. She may not like a lot of the staff that worked there, but she would always be loyal to Gregory. He had been her father's best friend growing up, until life drifted them apart. It was at her father's funeral that she met Gregory for the first time. He was genuinely saddened at his friend's death. At the wake, Vivian spoke with him at length, and they kept in contact for a couple of years. When Gregory called asking if she wanted to be his CFO, it was serendipity. She had recently lost her previous job and was glad to move to Cornwall where her father grew up.

Vivian pushed through the small crowd of people gathered around the bar. They all watched Lauren, who was now singing loudly out of tune to a Gloria Gaynor track. Vivian stepped in front of Lauren, grasping her flailing arm at the bicep. She took Lauren's fresh drink off her and placed it on the bar.

"Hey!" Lauren glared at the interruption. "Get off me."

Vivian held tighter, as Lauren tried to pull away. Lauren was a couple of inches taller than her own five-four. Lauren's hair had a messy but stylish look, cut just above her shoulders. Through the alcohol, Vivian detected hints of apple. A slow roll moved through her stomach, as Lauren's sky-blue eyes flashed with anger. *God, she's gorgeous.* Vivian shook the disquieting thought from her mind. "Come with me." She tugged Lauren's arm, surprised by the lack of resistance. She led Lauren through a back door and into the corridor that led to an emergency exit.

Lauren stopped, pulling her arm free. "Who are you?" she asked, her words slurring.

Vivian turned and glared at her. "I work for your father. I'm the CFO."

Lauren's gaze travelled over Vivian's body, her lips quirking into a grin. "It's about time Father hired himself some eye candy."

Vivian felt a red-hot rage course through her body. Her hands tightened into fists, trying desperately to curb the urge to slap her. It wasn't the first time Vivian had been called that, and it wouldn't be the last. She wasn't blind; she knew she was attractive. But having spent years trying to prove her brain was her best asset had been hard. At Bridger Holdings, she thought she had finally found a place to be comfortable in her own skin. Seeing Lauren leer at her the way some men did had angered her more than it should have.

"Don't ever speak to me like that again." Lauren flinched at the icy tone in Vivian's voice.

"I was just having some fun. Chill out. Jesus." Lauren backed up a step.

5

"What are you doing here?"

"It's the spring party, where else would I be?" Lauren fished a packet of cigarettes from her pocket and attempted to light one. Vivian snatched it out of her mouth.

"No smoking in here."

"It's my dad's business. I can do what I want." She put another one between her lips.

"It's illegal." Vivian snatched that one too, and the pack out of Lauren's other hand. She tossed the packet into the bin that stood near the exit.

"Spoilsport." Lauren stepped around Vivian. "I need a drink."

"Don't you think you've had enough?" Vivian reached out, grabbing her wrist and spinning her around, bringing their bodies within inches of each other. Lauren glared at her, then took a step forward, making Vivian back up until she hit the wall behind her. Vivian's heart rate tripled. Her pulse pounded in her ears. It wasn't just the alcohol that was intoxicating. She was transfixed by the ire flashing in Lauren's gaze. Lauren reached up, tracing Vivian's cheek with gentle fingers. Vivian's eyes went wide, when Lauren dipped her head and crushed their lips together in a searing kiss. She should have pushed Lauren away but couldn't. The raw passion and taste of her tongue glued her in place. Vivian gripped her shoulders, pulling her closer still. She hadn't been kissed this well in a very long time. She found she was starving for more. Lauren's hand somehow found its way under Vivian's blouse, tracing her stomach, inching higher to her breasts.

Vivian's eyes popped open at the first touch of fingers on her hardened nipple. She shoved Lauren away. "What do you think you're doing?" Her breathing was ragged, her stomach in knots. She swiped a hand over her mouth. *I can't believe I just did that.* "How dare you do that to me."

"I didn't hear you saying no." Lauren inched forward. "Come back to my place. We can have a good time."

Vivian narrowed her eyes, her anger returning full force. "If you think I'd go anywhere with someone as despicable and reckless as you, then you're stupider than you look."

Lauren moved back, eyes wide. The momentary look of hurt was gone in a flash, replaced with her own anger. "Don't presume you know anything about me." She stepped forward and poked Vivian hard in the chest. "You were the one who had their hand down my trousers."

Vivian was about to refute the claim but stopped herself when she noticed her hand was damp. *I didn't do that, did I?* Her hand trembled with the urge to bring her fingers to her nose to check if it was true. *How could I have touched her like that and not even realised?* She tightened the guilty hand into a fist. She wouldn't give Lauren the satisfaction. *How could I do that to Gregory's daughter?* Shame washed over her. *I'm going to lose my job.* Her fear must have been apparent. Lauren relaxed her stance and eased the space between them.

"Don't worry. I won't tell Father you wanted to fuck his daughter in a back corridor."

"I didn't. I don't."

"You're a liar, but whatever. I have to go."

Lauren turned away and walked toward the fire exit. Vivian stood against the wall, chest heaving. *What have I done?* She righted herself and headed back into the function room. She grabbed a wine from a passing bartender, swigging it down in four long gulps.

"Vivian. There you are."

Vivian coughed the last mouthful down at hearing Gregory's voice. He'd been absent from the party so far. Vivian was glad he wasn't around to witness Lauren making a fool of herself. *Or the episode in the corridor.* She turned to greet him, consciously not holding her hand out to shake his. "Gregory, you did it again."

Gregory glanced around the hall at the decorations and the staff, his eyes full of joy. "It has been another great year. And long may it continue." He reached into his pocket and pulled out an envelope. "I meant to give this to you earlier, but with the final preparations for tonight, I forgot." He handed the envelope over. "It's your bonus for a job well done."

Vivian didn't open it. How could she, when she had just had her hand in his daughter's underwear? "Thank you, Gregory. You made it easy." She smiled at him and hoped it came off as sincere. Inside, she was dying. "I'm terribly sorry, but I'm going to have to call it a night."

"Oh?" Gregory raised his bushy brows. At sixty-four, he was still a handsome man. "I was hoping to steal a dance with you."

"That's very sweet, but with a new year comes a new budget. I want to get an early start on the projections."

"Duncan would have been so proud of you," he said, alluding to her father.

"I hope so."

Gregory leaned in, hugging her tightly. "You're a remarkable woman. I'm so pleased you decided to join us four years ago."

I used to feel the same. I'm not so sure anymore. As he pulled back and stepped away, Vivian's shame overwhelmed her. *Of all the people to make out with, I had to do it with bloody Lauren Bridger.* She just hoped she wouldn't be seeing Lauren ever again. It was highly unlikely. They hadn't met in the previous years, no reason to think their paths would cross again in the future. *A fool's hope. It's sod's law she'll be back again sooner than I'd like.*

CHAPTER ONE

Eight months later...

"You know, this is a good business plan, Dad." Lauren paced her father's office. She couldn't understand why he was being so obtuse. She had done her research, spent three months gathering all the necessary paperwork. *Why is he making this so damn hard?* She knew why. They had never gotten along. Gregory always preferred his son. She supposed choosing to live with her mother when they split up hadn't helped. Celeste Bridger had walked away from Gregory, taking nothing with her. She didn't even ask for anything in the divorce. She had just wanted to get away from him. Lauren understood. He spent so much time at work, he never paid his wife any attention. Especially when his business took off and he spent all his time chasing contracts and clients. In the end, it had been all too much for Celeste. She packed a bag and moved back to France when Lauren was eleven years old. Damien, Lauren's brother, had been fifteen and stayed to work with their father. Gregory had demanded Lauren stay in England, but Celeste wouldn't allow it. That was fine with Lauren. She loved her mother. There was no other place she would rather be than by her side. Lauren could only assume this was why Gregory was practically forcing her to beg for the loan. She wanted to open her own chain of health clubs, complete with gyms, spas, and treatments. To do that, she needed capital. Her father was the only option for a loan. She didn't want the funds for a whole chain, just enough to start the first one. *Surely with all his money, that isn't too much to ask for.* He was a multimillionaire and could easily afford the £850,000 she needed.

"You're asking for a lot of money," Gregory replied, his lips pulled up into a grim smirk.

"I know, but it'll be worth it." Lauren stopped her pacing and looked out his office window. Her gaze found the sea on the horizon. It was a nice view from the twentieth floor. She had always loved the ocean and dreamed of one day settling down by the beach. *Find the right woman, maybe get a dog.* She turned her attention back to Gregory. "I've got everything lined up; the permits, business licence, insurance, it's all good to go. I just need the capital."

"If it's such a good idea, why not go to the bank?"

"You know damn well they won't give it to me. I have nothing to borrow against and no funds of any kind, not anymore." Spending the last few years out of the country hadn't helped her any for her future endeavours. But she didn't regret the choices she'd made. She would do them all again in a heartbeat. Her mother deserved to be looked after. Lord knows Gregory never bothered to help out. She had spent the last of her savings paying the architect and for the planning permits. All she needed now were the funds to start remodeling the property she had found.

"Yes. They'd be a fool to lend you that kind of money." He leaned forward in his chair, pinning Lauren with a glare.

"Is that how you see me? A fool."

"That's not fair."

Gregory blew out a breath and relaxed his posture. For a moment, a glimpse of the father she used to know shone through. "You're right, I'm sorry. But Lauren, you're asking for up to a £1,000,000. That's a lot of money to pull out of my business in the hope your idea works. I'm not sure I want to take that kind of risk."

"You did for Damien." Gregory had given Damien £5,000,000 to start his own yacht making business, and yes, it was successful. So could Lauren's idea. As much as she hated asking, she had no choice.

"Damien worked for me since he was a boy. I know his work ethic is solid."

"So, you're saying because I never worked here, you can't trust me?" *Or is it because I chose Mother over you?* Lauren sat in the guest chair, exhausted by this whole thing. She had only been in there fifteen minutes, and she already couldn't wait to get away from him.

"Your words, not mine." Gregory pressed his intercom. "Felicia, can you send in Vivian, please."

Lauren frowned, turning her head as his office door opened. A petite, dark-haired woman walked in, and a feeling of déjà vu settled in her gut. Lauren took in the tailored trouser suit, chestnut wavy hair, and chocolate eyes. She was sure they had met before but couldn't place the woman. *Probably seen her around here at some point.* The woman, Vivian, went to Gregory's side, her gaze looking over Lauren's shoulder, almost like she was afraid to look directly at her.

"Lauren, this is Vivian Westfall, my CFO. I asked her to look over your proposal."

"Why?"

"She's the money lady. Every financial decision I make has her approval. I trust her."

Vivian cleared her throat, her cheeks tinting pink. "Hello, Ms. Bridger."

"Have we met?" Lauren narrowed her eyes, as a prickling sensation ran down her spine. *I definitely know her.*

"Um, no." Vivian cleared her throat. "No, we haven't."

"Vivian, did you look over the proposal?"

"I did, Gregory. Ms. Bridger did a very good job putting it all together."

"What are your thoughts?"

"Well, I'd like to look into things a little more thoroughly, but providing her research and paperwork all checks out, I don't see why investing should be a problem."

Lauren shot to her feet. "Investing? I don't want an investment. I need a loan." No way she wanted her father in any way involved with her business. She wanted the cash, not a tie to him.

"Lauren, if you think for one minute I'm going to loan you money without making back anything in return, then you're sadly mistaken. I'll want the loan repaid monthly, with five percent of the profits."

"But it's my business."

"I won't interfere with the running of things, but I will want dividends."

Lauren glared at him, hating the grin he sported. She didn't have a choice. If she wanted to get the business off the ground, she would have to go along with him. She planned on the venture doing well, if she had to give him a cut, then so be it. She sat back down. "Fine."

"There's one more thing."

"What?"

"If I go ahead with this, I'll want someone with you while you get things set up, and for the first couple of months of opening."

"I don't need a babysitter." Now she was getting pissed off. *Why is he doing this to me?* They may not be as close as they once were, but she was still his daughter. *Why can't he trust me?*

"If you want my money, you'll do as I request."

He had her backed into a corner. "Who?"

"Vivian."

Vivian's eyes went wide, a look of panic flashing in her gaze. Lauren wondered what her problem was. For a suit, she was pretty enough. Older than Lauren's thirty-six by about five years. Under different circumstances, Lauren might have asked her out. It wasn't easy to tell she was a lesbian, but Lauren spotted the signs. She idly wondered if Gregory knew. *Probably not. He didn't exactly take my coming out so well.* Being from the older generation, he couldn't understand it all. Their relationship had always been strained, but her coming out had worsened things. He never mentioned it, never asked if she was seeing anyone, and frankly, Lauren didn't care. She had no desire to share anything with him.

"Gregory, with all due respect, I can't just uproot my life for months to live across the country. And what about my job here?"

"Vivian, your job here is safe. You can work remotely from up there. I want you with Lauren to make sure my investment is safe."

"I know what I'm doing," Lauren ground out. She may not have been involved in his business, but that didn't mean she hadn't picked up a thing or two. The night classes she took in France helped. She had no reservations about her competence in making this work.

"I'm sure you think so. However, until I'm positive you're not going to blow hundreds of thousands of pounds, I want Vivian with you." He looked up at Vivian, who still had a deer-in-the-headlights look. "Vivian?"

"Where would I stay?"

"I'll rent somewhere nice for you, all expenses paid. You won't need to worry about a thing, except keeping an eye on the numbers. So, what do you say?"

Vivian glanced at Lauren, her blush returning. "I appreciate your faith in me, Gregory. I won't let you down."

"Do I get a say in this?"

"Of course you do. You either accept my terms or try to find someone else willing to give you the capital you need."

"Not much of a choice." She folded her arms across her chest, resisting the urge to pout.

"Don't sulk, Lauren. This is business, pure and simple. I didn't get this far in life by throwing money away."

"Fine."

"Excellent. I'll have my solicitor draw up a contract."

"Great. I'll see you later." She needed to get out of there. She'd always hated his claustrophobic office. The dark wood and grotesque artwork made her stomach roll.

She barrelled through the door and headed to the lift. *Time for a swim. I need to burn my irritation off.* She should be happy. She now had the money to make a new life, to get away from Cornwall once and for all. She would have liked to stay in France, but there were too many memories of her mother there. No, she needed a fresh start, somewhere no one knew her.

The lift doors opened. She stepped inside and pressed the button for the lobby. As the doors began to close, an arm poked through and stopped them. Vivian joined her, slightly out of breath.

"Ms. Bridger, can I have a word?"

"What?" The doors closed and they descended.

"If this is going to be awkward for you, I'm sure I can talk your father into not letting me go."

Lauren noticed the woman shifting from foot to foot. "Why would it be awkward?"

"You don't remember me, do you?"

"Should I? I thought we hadn't met."

Vivian glanced away, her forehead creasing as she frowned. "We haven't."

She's lying. "Then why would it be awkward?" Lauren narrowed her eyes, trying desperately to remember her. She knew they had met somewhere before, and not just in passing. Something about Vivian was comforting, as though she somehow soothed Lauren's soul.

"I just meant, erm, about you feeling like you're being babysat."

"Don't worry about me. That's just my father's way of reminding me of my place in the world. It's all about control with him."

Vivian frowned again. "That doesn't sound like Gregory."

"Then you don't know him very well. He hasn't given me a penny my whole life." The lift doors opened, and Lauren stepped out, striding away. Vivian kept pace beside her.

"I thought he paid for you to go travelling these past few years?"

Lauren stopped, shaking her head and blinking in disbelief. "Who the hell told you that? That's laughable. The last thing he paid for was a birthday cake for my ninth birthday." She started walking again, toward the opulent revolving doors. *Everything here is so gaudy.*

"Then where have you been all these years?" Vivian called out.

Lauren blew out a breath and went back to Vivian, her frustration growing. She just wanted to get out of there. "Why all the questions?"

"Just curious." Vivian shrugged.

"That's how gossip starts." Lauren thought about not answering, but she could see genuine interest in Vivian's

17

gaze. "If you must know, I spent five years in France helping out my mother until she died of complications caused by Alzheimer's."

"Oh, God." Vivian reached out, touching Lauren's arm. "I'm so sorry. I had no idea. Gregory never said."

"Why would he? They divorced when I was eleven. He didn't even bother coming to the funeral, too busy planning his next big party." In two months, it would be the first anniversary of her death. After Celeste died, Lauren came home in a state. She had spent weeks drinking every night to drown out her grief, sleeping with strangers, and generally making an ass out of herself. It wasn't until she went to her father's spring party that things came to a head. She hadn't wanted to go, but she thought connecting with Gregory again might start mending their relationship. It didn't work. He had greeted her in his office with a kiss on the cheek and that was that. She went down to the convention hall, where the party was in full swing, and preceded to get very drunk. She'd even made out with a hot woman in a hallway.

Lauren blinked, her heart pounding in her chest. *It was you.* She was sure she felt the colour drain from her face. Vivian must have noticed her shock. She narrowed her eyes and reached out again. Lauren took a step back to stop Vivian touching her. She could recall exactly how Vivian's hand had felt on her skin. She didn't need a physical reminder.

"What is it?" Vivian asked, still squinting at her.

"Nothing." That night had been the worst of her life. Lauren remembered kissing Vivian, who called her despicable, reckless, and stupid. That was the last time she'd had a drink. She didn't want to be seen that way. Especially

18

by someone as put together as Vivian Westfall. *She had her hand in my trousers.* Lauren may have been drunk, but she remembered being the most turned on she had been in a very long while. *She must remember me. That's why she wants out. Probably afraid I'll jump on her again.* Lauren couldn't speak, her embarrassment from that night rearing its head. "I gotta run. You should start getting your affairs in order if you're moving to Scotland for the foreseeable future. I want to make a start first of January." That gave her three weeks to get Christmas over with and pack up the flat she had been renting since she moved back from France.

"Why there?"

"I don't know why you keep on with the questions. It's none of your business." Lauren turned to escape, but Vivian grabbed her hand. The touch caused Lauren's skin to heat.

"It is my business. I'm being made to relocate for God knows how long. I deserve to know."

"Fine. It's the farthest away I could get from here." She motioned around the building with her other hand.

"I don't understand. If you hate your father so much, why ask him for a loan?"

"He's the only person willing to give me the money. I want to have a career, a business of my own. As they say, it's better the devil you know." She pulled her hand free. "Are we done now? Or do you want to know my shoe size and the name of my first pet?"

Vivian nodded. "We're done."

"Good." She didn't mean to sound so surly. On the heels of dealing with her father, remembering Vivian's hands on her and the way her lips tasted, had her nerves jangling. She needed to get out of there, away from the memories.

"January first, don't forget. Plan to be in Scotland before the new year."

"What if I have plans?"

"Do you?"

Vivian shook her head. "Not anymore."

"Good." With that, Lauren turned on her heel, buttoned her coat, and headed out into the chill winter afternoon.

CHAPTER TWO

Vivian pulled in a deep breath, as she watched Lauren stride across the street. "Shit." When Gregory had asked her to look over his daughter's business proposal, her heart nearly gave out. Eight months hadn't been nearly enough time to erase the night of the party from her mind. She could still clearly remember every second of their interaction. *Except how my hand got down her pants.* Spending the next few months working closely with her was not something she was looking forward to. Despite the fact Vivian found her insanely attractive, Lauren was the boss's daughter and quite clearly filled with anger. Vivian didn't relish the thought of having to deal with her tantrums on a daily basis. She was just glad Lauren didn't remember her.

21

Vivian took the lift back up to her office, opposite Gregory's on the twentieth floor. She settled behind her desk and pulled out a pad of paper from the drawer. She needed to make a list of everything she needed to get done before her move. She would also need to call her sister to tell her she wouldn't be making the New Year's party she had planned. She had just finished jotting down the last item when there was a knock at her door. She looked up and saw Gregory standing at the threshold. He smiled warmly at her.

"Are you busy?" he asked, stepping into the room.

"Always. But for you, I can spare a minute or two."

He chuckled as he sat in the leather guest chair. "You're such a charming woman, Vivian. I'm surprised you're still single."

"I work too much to find time for dating."

"I could offer to cut back your hours, but I'm afraid I'm too selfish and need you here."

Vivian waved him off. "I wouldn't want you to. Dating only leads to heartache." Her last relationship ended the day she walked out of her old position. She told everyone it was because of budget cuts, but the real reason was because of Lesley Tanner. Lesley was the CEO she had been dating. That sordid affair taught Vivian to never get involved with someone you worked with. She had lost her job, because she had allowed the sweet nothings Lesley whispered in her ear to tempt her into an affair. *I won't make that mistake again.* That was one of the reasons she kept her life private at Bridger Holdings.

"I'd agree with you, but nothing quite compares to the blossoming of love."

Gregory looked wistful, and Vivian wondered who he was thinking of. She realised then she didn't really know him. Although they got on well and had mutual respect for one another, their lives rarely crossed outside work.

"I wanted to talk to you about Lauren," Gregory said, pulling his attention back to Vivian. "I know this came out of the blue for you, and I'm sorry you have to change your life for a while. But there is no one else I trust to keep an eye on her. I'm sure you'll be back in a few weeks anyway. I can't see her sticking this out."

Vivian raised her brows, not sure she was hearing right. "Are you saying you're expecting her to fail?"

"Why yes. You don't think this stupid idea of hers will work, do you?" Gregory laughed. "Vivian, just because she spent a couple of weeks putting together this fancy business plan, doesn't mean it'll succeed."

Vivian knew that wasn't true. She had spent hours looking over everything Lauren had compiled. Lauren had done a very professional job, and it certainly would have taken much longer than two weeks to complete. She had detailed plans drawn up and secured permits and the like. It wouldn't surprise Vivian if this had taken months of works. She even had a crew lined up that were willing to start on the first of January. That alone would have taken some doing. Not many people were willing to work on a bank holiday. Vivian wouldn't have suggested Gregory invest if she didn't think it would be successful.

"I don't understand. If you think it will fail, why agree to advance her the money?"

Gregory leaned forward in his chair, resting his forearms on her desk. "Lauren and I have a very complicated

relationship. I've seen her a handful of times over the last
few years. We're not close. I'd like to be a proper father to
her. Despite her being in her thirties, she'll always be my
little girl. If I have to lose some money to show her I'm not
the monster she thinks I am, so be it. In a month or two,
when the project falls flat, at least I can say I believed in her
and tried to help."

*But you don't believe in her. How is it I have more faith
in her than you do?* "Gregory, I think you're being a little
hard on her. The business plan is solid. I really think it will
work."

Gregory straightened in his chair, his gaze thinning
slightly. "We'll see. Anyway, as I said, I trust you to keep an
eye on her and my money. Make sure she doesn't squander
my investment. I'm willing to lose some of it, but not all. If
you think she's making poor decisions, call me and I'll rein
her in."

"You want me to be a go-between? To spy on her?"

"You make it sound so nefarious." He waved his hand. "I
simply want you to make sure she doesn't blow all my cash.
It's no different from what you do here daily."

Vivian wasn't so sure about that. It was clear he wanted
her to watch Lauren closely and report back to him. She
could read between the lines, and she wasn't happy about it. *I
won't be a pawn in their game.* She smiled at him. "I'm sure
you'll have nothing to worry about, but if something comes
up, I'll let you know."

"Good, that's all I ask." He stood from the chair. "Felicia
has made your travel arrangements. She's rented you a
holiday cottage on a month to month basis. I'm not sure

where Lauren plans to stay, but she's welcome to join you there if you don't mind a roommate."

So I can keep a closer eye on her, you mean. "Sounds great. I'll arrange a meeting with her for some time in the week to iron out the details."

"Thank you, Vivian. I'll leave you to your work. Before you head up there, meet with Jerry. He'll give you a company computer to take with you, so you can log on to the network."

"Okay." Vivian's laptop was more than capable of handling all of Bridger Holdings' business, but Gregory was a stickler for security and would only allow a company PC to handle his accounts.

After he left, she glanced back over her list. She tried to concentrate on the things she needed to get done, but thoughts of Lauren kept intruding. Despite Gregory's words, it was clear he didn't trust her. *Lauren was right, I don't know him at all.* She had a feeling she was going to get into the middle of a family drama she had no urge to be in.

†

Later that evening, Vivian knocked on her neighbour's door. Annie had moved next door just over a year ago, and in that time, they had become good friends. Annie was probably the only friend she had. Of course she had acquaintances, people she could go for a drink with, but she wasn't as close to them as she was with Annie. That was only because Annie lived right beside her and was very outgoing. The first day she moved in, she had come over to Vivian's to introduce herself and stayed for two hours. Their friendship had grown, and she was the only person, aside from family, that Vivian trusted.

"Hey, Viv." Annie was in her mid-thirties, with thick, strawberry red hair that reached her hips. They were about the same height, but Annie was a good ten pounds lighter. Vivian supposed that was due to running around after her three rambunctious kids. Working long hours at the office left Vivian no time for exercise. "What's up?" Annie asked.

"Do you have time for a chat?"

"Of course."

Annie stepped away from the threshold. They headed into the lounge, and Vivian instantly felt calmer. Annie had a fire roaring in the fireplace. The heat was just right for this cold December night. Vivian shed her jacket, laying it over an armchair. She settled onto the couch next to Annie.

"I don't know where to start." Vivian's thoughts all collided at once. "I need you to keep an eye on my house for a few months."

"How come?"

"I'm moving up north for work."

Annie's brows pinched as she squinted at Vivian. "Gregory doesn't usually send you away. What's going on?"

"I won't technically be working for Gregory. He's investing in his daughter's new business venture and wants me to keep an eye on the finances."

Annie eyed her for a moment, her lips pulled between her teeth as she thought. "Are you talking about Lauren?"

"I'm surprised you remember her name."

"Viv, honey, the night you came home from the party, you were a mess. You thought, for sure, you'd be fired if he found out." Annie reached out and laid her hand on Vivian's thigh. "How could I forget the name of the woman who caused you so much distress?"

Distress was the right word. After leaving the party, Vivian had come straight here. She fell into Annie's arms and wept as she explained what happened.

"I seem to remember that no other woman had turned you on so much before and you were worried you'd lose your job." Annie's advice had been to forget it ever happened, something Vivian couldn't do. She had replayed that scene over in her mind so many times she could recount exactly how many buttons were on Lauren's shirt.

Vivian nodded. "Yes, it's her. I don't think she remembers me, so that's good. But Gregory wants me to keep an eye on her. He practically told me to spy."

"I don't understand. What's his issue with her?"

"I don't exactly know what's gone on. From what I can gather, their relationship is strained. He doesn't trust her but wants her to think that he does."

"What will you do?"

Vivian smiled. "Why do you think I came here? I need your advice."

Annie glanced away, clicking her tongue. "Well, what do you think of her idea?"

"I think it's really good. I can't see why it would fail. Unless she's a complete idiot, it should be successful."

"And how do you feel about working closely with her?"

"Terrified." Vivian's skin heated, as she recalled the party again. "She has this magnetism to her. I worry I'll be drawn to her even more. Annie, I can't sleep with the boss's daughter."

"You are in a pickle, aren't you?"

Vivian blew out a frustrated breath. "That's not helpful."

"I know. I'm thinking." Annie stood and paced a small circle, gazing up at the ceiling. "If you're there to keep an eye on the money, how much contact would you need to have with her?"

Vivian shrugged. "Not much. Most of my work will be done in the place I'm staying."

Annie stopped her pacing. "Well, there you go. Just stay away from her. You can't get freaky if you're not together."

"Are you forgetting Gregory wants me to report back to him? Just because I shouldn't see her, doesn't mean that he won't order me to. He'll probably want me on her tail all day. And let's not forget, she could remember that night at any moment. What then?"

"You'll be embarrassed." Annie sat back down. "I'm sorry, Viv. I have no advice to give. You're obviously attracted to her. I say go for it. Forget what Gregory thinks."

Vivian shook her head. No way she would ever admit her attraction to Lauren. Add to that, she loved her job at Bridger Holdings; she wouldn't do anything to jeopardise her position there. She also didn't want to spy on Lauren. She was stuck in the middle, whether she liked it or not.

"This sucks. I know what Gregory wants me to do, but I can't do that to her." Vivian gazed at the fire. "There's something about her, Annie. After the meeting with her father, we spoke for a few minutes. She was all angry and frustrated, and it was clear she didn't hold Gregory in high regard. She told me her mother recently died of Alzheimer's." She looked back at Annie. "You should have seen her face when she told me. She looked heartbroken. For whatever reason, she and Gregory don't get on, but I can't see that being all her fault. She looked so lost, out of place in the world. I want to help her."

"But you don't want to let Gregory down."

"No. What am I going to do?"

Annie lifted her arm and pulled Vivian into a side hug. "We've circled back to your original question, and unfortunately, I don't have the answer. All I can say is do what's in your heart. You're a good person, Viv. When the time comes, you'll make the right decisions."

"I hope so."

Vivian hadn't got the answers she was looking for, but at least she knew when the shit hit the fan, Annie would have her back. I guess that's something. I just pray everything goes smoothly and I won't have to make a choice that will destroy my career, or Lauren's trust in people.

CHAPTER THREE

Vivian sipped her coffee, as she waited for Lauren to show up. It was Thursday evening and they had arranged to meet in the pub closest to Bridger Holding's office block. Vivian would have preferred to meet somewhere less intimate, and during the day. Sitting beside a roaring fire, nestled in a quiet corner, it looked like she was waiting on a date. In the days since chatting to Annie, Vivian still hadn't come up with any ideas on how to handle the situation. Her best hope was that Lauren did a brilliant job in opening the health club, so Vivian wouldn't need to report back to Gregory.

She scanned the folder on the table in front of her, looking over Lauren's timeline for the build and subsequent opening. If they ran on time, Vivian wouldn't be back until late spring. *Four months. How am I going to work with her for four months? And not forgetting Gregory wants me to stay after to make sure it runs smoothly.* Her attraction to Lauren lingered in the pit of her stomach. Despite Lauren's apparent anger at the world, there was just something about her that captivated Vivian. She wanted to get to know Lauren better but feared her interest would jeopardise her job at Bridger Holdings. She wasn't prepared to do that. *No. Best I put any thoughts about Lauren and I becoming friends to the back of my mind. It'll only lead to trouble.*

"Hey."

Vivian gasped and looked up. She had been so wrapped up in her thoughts, she hadn't heard Lauren slide into the opposite seat. Lauren's hair was windswept, and dark circles ringed her eyes. It was clear she hadn't been sleeping. Vivian wanted to ask if she was okay but bit her lip. It wasn't any of her business.

"Good evening, Ms. Bridger. Thank you for meeting with me."

"Call me Lauren. And no problem. Did Dad give you the schedule?"

Vivian lifted the piece of paper. "Yes. It's pretty tight. Are you confident you can get this done on time? And on budget?"

Lauren narrowed her eyes, her hand sweeping her hair back from her face. "Not you, too."

"What?"

"I don't know what my father told you, but I know what I'm doing. I don't need second-guessing."

"Hey, calm down. I wasn't second-guessing you. My job is to keep an eye on the finances. I need to know if there will be any problems."

Lauren grinned, shaking her head. "Let's not play games. I know exactly why you're coming up with me."

Vivian's heart rate picked up. She cleared her throat. There was no way Lauren knew what Gregory had asked of her. She schooled her expression, years of boardroom work lending itself to her poker face. "I have no idea what you're talking about."

Lauren leaned in, her gaze predatory. "My father doesn't trust me. He thinks this will fail. He's sending you to watch me. To report back to him. And if I know my father, he wants you to keep an eye on my personally, to make sure I'm not out to make trouble for him."

"That's not true."

"You're lying." Lauren shifted in her seat, crossing her ankle over her knee. She relaxed her features, her smile more genuine now. "Listen, it's fine. I know how he operates. He did the same to my brother when he invested in his yacht business. Dad doesn't trust anyone. If he wants to send a guard dog to keep an eye on me, then so be it. I don't intend to fail. I know my plan is solid. If he wants to waste your time watching me, that's up to him."

Vivian was at a loss. She never expected Lauren to know Gregory's true motives. In a way, she was glad Lauren knew. At least now Vivian didn't feel like she was lying to her. But it didn't change the fact Vivian was still expected to spy on her. There was no point denying the accusation. "You're right, Ms. Bridger, that is what he wants. But don't presume that is what I intend to do." Vivian thought it best to be honest from the outset. If they were going to be spending the next few months together, starting on the right foot would be wise. "For your information, what I said in Gregory's office is true. I think your business plan is great. I see no reason why it wouldn't be successful. I fully support this and want to help in any way I can."

Lauren narrowed her gaze again. "You look sincere enough, but, like my father, I don't trust anyone. You're my father's right-hand woman. You'd probably say anything to get me onside."

Vivian shrugged. "Believe what you want. I only want to do my job and help you make this a success."

"Time will tell." Lauren leaned forward. "But I'm warning you now, I don't take kindly to being stabbed in the back."

The intensity in Lauren's gaze caused Vivian to shift slightly in her seat. *How is it, when she looks so fierce like that, she turns me on?* Lauren was belligerent and full of anger. This wasn't the type of woman Vivian should even give a second thought to, but she couldn't stop herself from wondering how Lauren would look in the throes of passion.

"I reiterate, I'm here to do a job. If I think for one second Gregory's money is at risk, I won't hesitate to pull the plug." She sipped her coffee. "Now, tell me about the timeline."

Lauren glared at her for a moment longer, then stood and headed to the bar.

She came back a few minutes later with a bottle of beer. She took a long pull of the drink, then swiped the back of her hand across her lips. "The money has been transferred to the landowner, so the property is now mine. The architect I hired has the plans finalised. His builders are ready to start tearing down the old façade January first. I've got the permits and insurances taken care of. I've spent all my savings getting this started. Everything is set. Barring unforeseen circumstances, there shouldn't be any trouble finishing on time. All I need is the account information so I can make the payments to the team. The contractors aren't happy about starting on a bank holiday, but I've promised them a good bonus upfront to get them to work on the first."

"Gregory has opened a company account for the project, but it's in my name."

Lauren shook her head and took another swig of her beer. "He really doesn't trust me, does he?" Her voice cracked. She looked down at the table, biting her lower lip.

Without thinking, Vivian reached across the table and grasped Lauren's hand, the feel of her skin soft and cool. "I'm sorry."

Lauren smiled sadly, squeezing Vivian's fingers. "It's okay. It's always been that way."

"Can I ask why?"

"I wouldn't know where to start." Lauren pulled her hand free, blowing out a breath. "We've had a lot of issues over the years, but the main problem is I chose my mother over him. When they divorced, my mother moved back to France. He told her my brother and I would stay here with him. I didn't want that. I was eleven years old. I wanted my mother. She wanted me too. I don't think he ever forgave me for choosing her over him."

Vivian knew there was more to the story. Lauren wouldn't make direct eye contact and that action alone was enough to pique Vivian's interest. She wanted to delve deeper but knew it wasn't her right to ask. "Lauren, you were a kid. Surely he can't hold that against you."

"This is Gregory Bridger we're talking about. Nobody says no to him, especially his family. Mum was so desperate to get away from him, she left with nothing but her passport and her credit card. She didn't even ask for anything in the divorce."

Vivian couldn't reconcile Lauren's words to the man she had worked with for four years. Gregory had been nothing but kind and supportive toward her. He even came to the hospital when Vivian had her appendix removed. That didn't sound like the man Lauren was describing. Before she had a chance to comment, Lauren continued.

"I know this is hard to believe. He puts on a great show. But Vivian, he's not a nice man. At least not to most of the world."

"I've worked for him for years. I've never seen him be anything but gracious and kind."

Lauren sighed. "I can only tell you what I know and have seen with my own eyes. He may seem that way to you now, but there will come a day when you cross him. Then you'll see the true Gregory Bridger."

Vivian thought over Gregory's words after the meeting they had. He said himself he didn't trust Lauren, but he also said he wanted to be a good father to her. *A good father wouldn't send someone to spy on their daughter.* Vivian's thoughts were too jumbled and conflicted to make any sense.

"Why take his money?"

"I told you before, better the devil you know." Lauren finished her beer. "Now, about travel arrangements. I assume he found you somewhere nice and fancy to stay while up there."

Vivian nodded. "He's rented a cottage near the job site. He, uh, did say it was a two-bedroom place, and that you could stay there too."

"Easier to keep an eye on me." Lauren grinned.

"There's no point in lying. That's what I thought."

"Well, I want this project to go ahead with as little interference from him as possible. If it's all right with you, I'll take you up on the offer. I was going to crash on one of the builder's couches. A nice cosy cottage sounds much better."

Not too cosy, I hope. The last thing Vivian wanted was to be spending cold, winter nights trapped in a cottage with Lauren Bridger. The more she got to know her, the more intrigued Vivian became. "I'll be driving up December thirtieth. That'll give me time to get settled and find my bearings."

"Sounds good. I'll meet you there." Lauren stood. "I hope my dad doesn't make this too hard for you."

Vivian stood also. "I'm sure it'll be fine. As long we stick to the budget and get the project finished on time, he won't have anything to complain about."

"We both know that's not true." Lauren held out her hand. "See you in a couple of weeks."

Vivian grasped her hand and gave it a shake. "See you soon." Vivian sat back down after Lauren walked away, her hand still warm from Lauren's touch. *This is going to be a cluster fuck.*

†

Lauren rounded the corner of the pub and walked up the alley beside it. She leaned against a wall, fishing a cigarette out of her pocket. She placed it between her lips but did not attempt to light it. She had been smoke free for three months but still found comfort in feeling the butt between her lips. She didn't indulge often, only when she was stressed. And sitting across from Vivian Westfall was stressful. She was just as beautiful as Lauren remembered. Long chestnut hair, pulled back into a professional ponytail, lent an air of authority to Vivian's presence. Her gaze was shrewd, seemingly able to stare into the depths of Lauren's soul. It had been that way the first time they met at the spring party. That night still replayed itself in Lauren's mind on a constant loop. Living and working with Vivian for the next few months was going to be torture. It wasn't often that Lauren felt drawn to someone. Having spent the last few years caring for her ailing mother had taken up all her time. The thought of meeting anybody wasn't in her immediate plans. Yes, she wanted to settle down with someone, but she didn't think that would be for years to come. Somehow though, Vivian had captured her attention. *How annoying is it that the first person to interest me works for my fucking father?*

She put the cigarette back into the packet and continued on her walk. Twenty minutes later, she unlocked the door to her studio apartment and tossed the keys onto the sideboard. Without turning on any lights, she went into the kitchen and pulled open the fridge. She took out a bottle of beer. She twisted off the cap, then sat at her small kitchen table in the dark living space. Her life was packed up into just three boxes. It wasn't much, considering she was thirty-six. She could easily fit all three boxes into her car and be in another part of the country overnight. It was depressing to think nobody would even miss her. She had a few acquaintances in France, but she hadn't even contacted them since arriving back in England. The only person she spoke to was Damien. They weren't as close as they once were as kids and it saddened her. In the ten months since she'd been home in the UK, she had only spoken to him a handful of times. She was alone.

Lauren chugged the beer, then threw the bottle in the rubbish. She grabbed all of the paperwork to do with the new project and carried the pile into the bedroom. She settled on the bed and spread out the papers. For the next two hours, she looked over everything she had prepared. Although she had told Vivian everything would be fine, that didn't stop her worrying that it might not be. She was determined to not let her father get the upper hand. She knew he was desperate for her to fail, despite loaning her the money. There had to be an ulterior motive, but she didn't want to think about that. She was going to make this work with as little input from Gregory as possible. Her only hope was that Vivian would stay out of the way. *And for that to happen I need to make sure everything runs smoothly.*

CHAPTER FOUR

Lauren looked around the perimeter of her father's grand living room. She hadn't been inside his house for over ten years. Nothing had changed. His awful taste in furnishings matched the design of his office block. Everything was dark, overly large, and gaudy. Her skin began to crawl, as the claustrophobia set in. Tonight, her father was throwing a small gathering to celebrate Christmas. Damien was there, along with her aunts and uncles, cousins, and a few business associates. She hadn't wanted to come, but he had demanded her presence, and she knew why. She had already been congratulated by many members of her family, extolling their happiness that father and daughter were reunited and that he was helping her to set up the business. She hated that he alluded to everyone that he was behind the project and doing her a favour. Many a time, over the evening, she had wanted to scream from the top of her lungs that it was all her idea. She was the one who had spent hour upon hour putting the proposal together. She had depleted her savings to pay the architect and secure the permits that were needed. But it was just like Gregory to take credit for it all.

Gregory tapped on his glass with a knife, hushing the din of the room. "Ladies and gentlemen, family and friends, colleagues. I would like to welcome you all to my home on this night of celebration. Tonight isn't just the annual Christmas gathering, it is also the night that my wayward daughter has found her way home." Lauren lowered her head. Too many pairs of eyes were glancing her way. Gregory continued. "As many of you know, I am taking great delight in helping Lauren on her new business venture. May it be a success." He raised his glass, his gaze boring into Lauren's. "To my beautiful daughter, welcome home." The guests all raised their glasses, and in unison echoed her father's words, "Welcome home".

Lauren gritted her teeth but dutifully raised her glass in thanks. She swallowed the champagne, then slammed her glass down onto the nearest surface. She needed some air. She ducked out of the living room, through the long hallway, and burst through the kitchen patio doors. Thankfully, the garden was empty. Lights were strung up around the trees bordering the neatly trimmed grass. The sound of a fountain trickling lent an air of calm to Lauren's beating heart. She fished her cigarettes out of her pocket and placed one between her lips. She lit this one. The first pull made her cough. By the third drag, she was smoking like a pro.

"Are you okay?"

Lauren glanced over her shoulder. Vivian stood only a few feet away. She looked gorgeous in her midnight-blue ballgown. Her hair was pinned on one side, flowing over her shoulder in a twist. Her arms were bare, save for a silver bracelet that reflected the moonlight. "I didn't know you were here." Lauren tried to keep her gaze on Vivian's eyes and not her cleavage.

"I come here every year. As much as I would rather be at home in my pyjamas and slippers, I need to show my support for your father." Vivian took another step forward, coming within inches of Lauren. "I heard what your father said, and what he has been telling people. I could tell by your face when you marched out of there that you weren't happy."

Lauren shrugged. She took another drag of the cigarette, careful to blow the smoke away from Vivian when she exhaled. "Of course I'm not happy. He's all but taken credit for the whole thing. It's not like I can disagree with him. He's the one who has the power to take my dream away." If she wasn't so filled with anger, Lauren may have broken down in tears. She wouldn't give him the satisfaction of knowing he had upset her. *One more week to go, and I will be in Scotland. Fingers crossed, I won't have to see him for a very long time.* She flicked the cigarette onto the floor and stubbed it out with her boot. It was then that she noticed Vivian shivering in the late December night. Without thinking, she removed her dinner jacket and placed it around Vivian's shoulders, gazing into her eyes.

"You'll freeze." Vivian's breath misted in the cold as she spoke.

"I'll be fine. I tend to run pretty hot." Lauren didn't miss the slight blush that covered Vivian's cheeks at her words. She stepped back, stuffing her hands into her trouser pockets. She stared at her father's house, rage burning in her gut. "I'm half tempted to quit the deal. I'm not sure I'm strong enough to be able to deal with him for however long it takes for me to pay him back."

"Lauren, I know how difficult this is for you, but you have to believe that it will be worth it." Vivian closed the distance between them and grasped Lauren's elbow. "I have looked over hundreds of business proposals in my time, and I can honestly say that yours is the most thorough and detailed plan I have ever seen. You have to stick with this, because I know it will work. You have a great mind and have worked so hard for this. Don't let the differences between you and your father stop you from achieving your goal."

"How can you say all that when you know he's out for me to fail?"

Vivian dropped her hand and blew out a breath. "Just because he believes you will fail doesn't mean that everybody else does. You have come so far. You have to do this."

Lauren tilted her head back, gazing up at the black, cloudless sky. Vivian's words swirled in her mind. She was right. If Lauren had any hope of moving on from her mother's death, and her father's disbelief in her, she would need to stick with the plan. She gazed back at Vivian, a small smile on her lips. "You're right, I need to do this. Are you all set and ready for the move?"

"Yes. Everything is packed. My neighbour will keep an eye on my house. All that's left is to pick up the computer equipment I'll need to work for Gregory up there."

Lauren nodded. "Cool. I guess I'll see you in a few days." She took a couple of steps away, then turned back around. "Thank you, Vivian, for giving me a pep talk and making sure I was okay. No one has believed in me since before my mother got sick. It feels nice." She turned and strode back through the patio doors, intent on leaving. Her father intercepted her by the large oak front door.

"Lauren, leaving so soon?"

Lauren smiled sweetly at him. "It's been a great party, but I have things I need to take care of before I leave for Scotland."

"I do hope everything goes well for you up there. Don't forget to keep me informed of my investment."

"You don't need to worry about that, Father, what with Vivian coming to keep an eye on me."

Gregory raised his eyebrows, his lips pulling up into a smirk. "Yes, my dear Vivian. Don't think I didn't see the little intimate conversation you had with each other outside. Of course, I don't know what was said, but I could see the interest in your gaze." He took a step forward, forcing Lauren to step back. "Keep your filthy hands off her. She isn't like you."

Lauren felt a chill run up her spine. It was then she noticed Vivian still had her jacket. As she glared at her father, his intentions were clear. Vivian was his. She briefly closed her eyes. Now she understood why Vivian thought Gregory was a nice man. He was trying to worm his way into her affections and was doing everything in his power to make her believe he was worthy of her. *But you're not, old man. She is as gay as the day is long.* If anybody had a chance with Vivian it would be Lauren. Not that Lauren was worthy, either. Vivian was in a class of her own. Elegant, authoritative, but also sweet and caring. All qualities of a woman who would want nothing to do with someone like Lauren.

"I have no intention of going after anybody who works for you. All I want is to get my business started."

Gregory stepped back and straightened his jacket. "Well, good luck with that. I'm sure you'll need it."

With that parting shot, he turned away from her and strode down the hallway and back into the living room. Lauren let out a breath, hating that he had witnessed the tender moment in the garden between her and Vivian. It had been a private conversation between the two of them. Gregory's witness tarnished the interaction. *Well, we've got four months to have plenty more exchanges that prick won't get to see.* She flung open the door and headed to her car. She was about to pull away, when there was a tap on the passenger side window. Damien stood beside the car. With his neatly trimmed hair slicked back and grey pinstripe suit, he looked like a character from a 1950s gangster movie. He opened the door and slid into the seat.

"Hey, Sis."

Lauren left the engine running, allowing the heaters to warm. She shifted her position, so she could see him. "Damien, how are you?"

"Doing really well, thank you." He took a long breath, his forehead creasing. "I couldn't help but overhear you and

Dad going at it again. Do you think you'll ever be on good terms?"

"I'm sorry, Damien, but I don't think so. I've tried hard over the years to make a connection with him, but he's just not interested."

Damien folded his arms across his chest, his lips pulled down into a frown. "I can't understand what his problem is. You're his daughter, for God's sake. Why does he have to be this way?"

Lauren shook her head. "I think he is still holding a grudge that I went to live with Mum." It was a good story. It sounded believable. Lauren hoped Damien would never find out the real truth as to why their father hated her so much. She would bear that secret for the rest of her life. There was no point dragging up the past. Damien certainly didn't need to know the truth.

"That can't be his only reason. I can understand why he would be hard on acquaintances if he doesn't get his way in business, but his own daughter? It just doesn't make sense."

"I don't think it ever will make sense. We are just two different people. It will probably always be this way." She hated lying to him, but it was her only option.

"Yeah, I guess so." Damien's frown turned into a grin, his eyes flashing happiness. "Congratulations, by the way, on your new venture. I'm sure you'll do amazing."

Lauren's grin matched his own. "It is pretty cool. I can finally start making something of myself."

"Lauren, you have always been something. Having a career and business won't change who you are inherently. There is nothing about you that needs upgrading."

"That's sweet of you to say, but I think Dad would have a different opinion."

"Who cares what he thinks? You don't need to prove yourself to anyone." He reached over and took her hand. "I'm sorry I couldn't invest when you asked me to. Sales are down recently, and I just couldn't work the figures into my budget."

"Damien, it's okay. I wouldn't want you to risk your own business in the hopes that mine might succeed."

"You *will* succeed. But just know that if you do need my help at any time, I'll be there for you."

"Thank you. That means a lot. And thank you for coming to the funeral."

"You don't need to thank me for that, she was my mother, too. I'm just sorry I didn't see her as much as I would have liked over the years."

Lauren wanted to be angry with her brother. In the years leading up to their mother's illness, Damien would visit two or three times a year. Once the Alzheimer's set in, there always seemed to be an excuse for him not to be able to make it. She never questioned why he didn't come. Sometimes it was hard to deal with the failing health of a parent. She would never begrudge him those feelings. That didn't mean she wasn't mightily pissed off dealing with everything on her own. That was one of the reasons why their relationship had become somewhat strained. She would always love her brother, but it would take time for their relationship to go back to how it was when they were kids.

"It's okay. By the end, she didn't even recognise me. She wouldn't have known who you were even if you had shown up."

"That's not the point. She was my mum. I should have been there."

Tears filled Damien's eyes. He covered his face with his hands as his shoulders shook. It was a bit disconcerting to see her forty-one-year-old brother crying. He hadn't even cried at the funeral. Lauren surmised these were tears of guilt. She did not attempt to comfort him, for this was his cross to bear in handling the situation the way he had. He brushed away the tears, breathing deeply a few times to calm himself.

"Sorry, Lauren, I don't know what came over me."

"It's fine. Don't worry about it."

"I have to get back to the party. You know what Dad is like if we're not all bowing down to his greatness."

Lauren was glad that Damien also saw their father the way she did. Despite Damien working for him for several years, he couldn't wait to get out from under his shadow. It would seem they had something in common. They were both happy to take money from their father, even though they both disliked him. *Does that make us bad people? Probably.* She shook the thought away. As her father had said in his office, this was business. She didn't have to like the people she was in business with.

Damien stepped from the car, said his goodbyes, and strolled back to the party. Lauren put the car in gear and pulled away. She hadn't planned on heading up to Scotland for another three days, but the thought of staying in Cornwall any longer made her nauseous. Nothing was keeping her. She would get a good night's sleep and be on the road first thing in the morning, ready to start her new life.

†

"Ah, Vivian, there you are." Gregory grasped Vivian's elbow, as she stepped back through into the kitchen. His eyes narrowed as his gaze swept over her body. "Isn't that Lauren's jacket?" He motioned with his head to the item in question, grasped tightly between Vivian's hands.

"Um, yes. We were outside discussing the project, and I was cold." Her hands gripped tighter as his gaze seemed to narrow even more. It was a look she hadn't seen before, and the glare made her uneasy. She had always been comfortable in his presence. He was like a second father to her, but their recent interactions had left her feeling somewhat disjointed. She could only assume it was because of the things Lauren had told her about him. She had never felt misgivings about him before, but now she looked at him in a new light. She still thought Lauren's words might come from a place of anger and might not be completely true. However, seeing this menacing scowl made her skin crawl. "She left before I had a chance to give it back to her. I'll take it with me to Scotland and return it then."

"While you are up there, don't forget to keep me updated." His hand went to the small of Vivian's back, guiding her up the hallway and into the living room. "Trust is a very fragile emotion. I would like to think our bond is indicative of that trust."

The hairs on Vivian's neck stood on end. It wasn't hard to miss exactly what it was he wanted her to do. From the moment he had asked her to keep an eye on Lauren, Vivian was wary. After speaking to Lauren, and experiencing Gregory's present behaviour, she realised just how much she didn't know him. Any woman with an ounce of sense would run for the hills. She should tell Gregory she wouldn't be a pawn in his game, and to find somebody else. But she needed her job, and she also didn't want anybody else reporting back on Lauren. Vivian was an honest person. She couldn't bear the thought of anybody else spying on Lauren, causing trouble between father and daughter. No, Vivian would be going to Scotland, but she wouldn't be spying. She would do what she had wanted to do all along, help Lauren to make this business venture a success.

Instead of replying to Gregory's thinly veiled threat, she said, "Why don't you go mix with your guests? I'm sure they are all desperate to talk to you."

Gregory's eyes lit up as his gaze scanned the room. "Yes, you're right. We can't have you monopolising all of my time, now can we?"

Vivian smiled as he walked away, the fake grin making her cheeks ache. As soon as he disappeared into the melee, she turned and went back into the hallway. She no longer wanted to be there. As she walked toward the front door, the pictures on the wall caught her attention. She had been in Gregory's house many times over the years but had never stopped to study the photos. There were six in total. There were three of Gregory and Damien fishing, and one of Damien as he cut the ribbon at the opening ceremony of his yacht building business. The main focus was an overly large, professional portrait of Gregory. The same image hung in the lobby of Bridger Holdings. The last picture was of a young woman cradling a baby. Above their heads hung a banner that read, *It's a Boy*. Vivian assumed this was Lauren's mother holding Damien. Vivian checked the other wall.

There are no other photographs. Lauren wasn't in any of them, not even as a young child. The only picture he had of her was the one in his office. *His hatred for Lauren must run deep. What on earth happened to cause their relationship to be like this? I'm not going to find out tonight. I'm not even sure I want to know.* It was clear Gregory disliked Lauren immensely, and Lauren wasn't too fond of him either. Vivian wondered again why Lauren would ask for money from him. Perhaps Lauren was right; it was better the devil you know. She wondered why he had a photo of Lauren in his office. *Probably for appearances sake.*

She retrieved her clutch from the sideboard and then pulled the door open. She stepped out into the cold night, her skin instantly chilling. Without giving it a thought, she threaded her arms through Lauren's jacket, pulling it tight around her waist. It was two sizes too big for her, but she found the extra material helped comfort her. The comfort certainly didn't come from the thought of it being Lauren's jacket that warmed her from the inside out. The softness of the cotton revealed how expensive the jacket was. Vivian rubbed her arms, the feel of the material reminding her of Lauren's skin. She dropped her arms, mentally rolling her eyes at how caught up with Lauren she was. She pulled the key from her clutch and unlocked the car. As she glanced over her shoulder back at Gregory's home, she saw him staring out at her through one of the downstairs windows. The sense of unease returned, and she quickly stepped into her car and pulled away. Although reticent to be moving to Scotland for so long, now she found she couldn't wait to get away. The thought of returning to Gregory's office made her stomach roll. She just hoped that by the time she got back, things would be back to normal. She knew that was a fool's hope. This project couldn't be over with soon enough.

CHAPTER FIVE

"You have reached your destination."

Vivian glanced at the GPS on the dashboard, as she rolled to a stop outside of a large, beautiful cottage. Flower boxes lined the gravel driveway, and pale blue shutters hung in the windows. It was seven o'clock in the evening, and although night had settled in, she could still see the exquisiteness of her new home. She was tired after driving for most of the day. All she wanted to do was drag her suitcases into her room, take a warm shower, and collapse into bed. Her plans would have to wait, as there was already a car in the driveway. Lauren had arrived first. Vivian had hoped to have a few hours to settle in by herself before having to face her.

Memories of their meeting at Gregory's Christmas party were still causing turbulence. Lauren had been angry and upset over Gregory's words, and Vivian couldn't blame her. It must be hard knowing that your father didn't trust you or see the value in you as a person. Vivian's relationship with her own father had been near perfect. He never missed a birthday, celebrated every big win in her career, and loved nothing better than visiting Vivian on Sunday afternoons and chatting about everything and nothing. Vivian couldn't imagine being estranged from him. He had been a loving and caring father. Vivian wished he were still alive.

She got out of the car and pulled her suitcases from the back seat, the computer equipment would remain in the boot overnight. Vivian had no plans of logging into the network until the morning anyway. She locked the car and headed up the walkway. She raised her hand and knocked on the door, wanting to give Lauren early warning of her arrival. She certainly didn't want to walk in and catch Lauren if she had just gotten out of the shower. The thought of Lauren freshly washed and still damp caused her stomach to tighten. She hadn't even seen her yet and already she was dreading the next few months. One thing about Vivian was that she was never afraid to go after what she wanted, especially in relationships. But there was no way she would be going after Lauren, no matter how attracted to her she was.

The door opened and Lauren's face came into view. She smiled and stepped back. "Hey, you made it. How was the drive?"

Vivian stepped over the threshold and into the living room, her skin instantly warming from the heat of the fireplace. She was surprised at the modern look the cottage had on the inside. She had expected old fashioned furniture and carpets. Instead, a leather couch and matching armchair, flooring tiles, and modern artwork encompassed the space. They were the kind of furnishings Vivian expected to see in an upscale apartment block. She put her suitcases down and turned to face Lauren. "It was long and boring. I felt for sure I was going to fall asleep along the way."

"Well, I'm glad you made it in one piece. I wasn't sure when you would be arriving, so I took the liberty of making a vegetable casserole. It's in the slow cooker in the kitchen when you're ready to eat. That's if you're hungry."

Vivian was touched that Lauren had taken the time to cook for her. She hadn't expected her to go through the trouble of making dinner. Then again, she hadn't expected Lauren to arrive until the next day. "That sounds heavenly. Thank you so much."

Lauren blushed, her ears tinting pink. She waved her hand dismissively. "No problem. Let me give you the grand tour."

Vivian followed, as Lauren led her through an archway. The same tile continued into the kitchen, gloss-white cabinets balanced black granite worktops. A small island stood in the middle. The aroma of the casserole simmering away caused Vivian's stomach to growl. She was ravenous and couldn't wait to get stuck in, but she dutifully followed Lauren around the rest of the cottage.

"Obviously, this is the kitchen. The owner stocked the cupboards and fridge with essentials, and I bought a few things on my way up here, enough to keep us going. We'll still need to go shopping sometime soon. This way to the bedrooms." Lauren led them from the kitchen and down a short hallway. The bathroom was at the end, again everything shiny and modern. Two doors stood either side of the corridor. One was open, and Vivian could see some of Lauren's clothing on the bed.

"I took the smaller room. I thought you would like the bigger room, as I know you will be working for my father while you're up here."

Vivian opened the door to the scent of fresh sheets assailing her nose. She stepped through, taking in the four-poster bed and quaint dresser. This was the only room that looked like country cottage living. There was a candlewick bedspread, a wicker chair, and a vase with wildflowers on the dresser.

"There is a large sideboard in the lounge, which I thought would be perfect for you to use as a desk. I spoke to the owner, she's happy for you to use it with a tablecloth to protect the surface."

"That'll be perfect. This place is pretty amazing."

"Do you think you will be comfortable here for the foreseeable future?" Lauren glanced at the floor as she asked the question. Vivian couldn't help but wonder if she was alluding to them cohabiting.

"Yes, I'm sure it will do nicely."

Lauren stuffed her hands into her pockets, clearing her throat. "I'll, uh, leave you to get settled. If you're not too tired, I was hoping we could go over tomorrow's schedule."

"Tomorrow is New Year's Eve. I thought you wanted to start on the first?"

"I do, but I was kinda hoping I could take you to the job site and show you the building we'll be renovating. I also

want to take a drive around the local area, show you why I
think this is the best place to start the business."
"I've read the business plan and seen your research; I
already know it's a good fit."
Lauren's blush returned. "I know, but there's nothing
quite like seeing it in person."
It was clear to Vivian that Lauren was eager to show off
her ideas. *I guess she hasn't had the chance to get excited
about this with anyone.* "I need to log into Bridger Holdings
first thing in the morning, but I suppose any time after ten
o'clock will be fine." She knew her reply sounded business
like, and she didn't miss the quick frown on Lauren's lips.
She didn't want to give Lauren the idea that they were
friends and this was a holiday. She was here to do a job. No
matter how much she wanted to get to know Lauren better,
she wouldn't allow it.
"Okay, great." Lauren's response lacked the enthusiasm
from a moment ago. "Help yourself to the casserole. I'm
going to take a shower and then see if there is anything good
on the TV."
Vivian watched her cross the hall and enter her room,
closing her door with a soft click. Vivian leaned back against
the bed, feeling like a jerk. She had hurt Lauren's feelings,
but there was nothing she could do. She wouldn't apologise
for keeping this professional.
She grabbed her suitcases from the living room and
unpacked her things. She slipped into jogging bottoms and a
fleece T-shirt, then went in search of the casserole. She sat at
the kitchen island as she ate. The casserole was delicious.
Lauren had done an amazing job. Vivian went back for
second helpings, the sound of the TV in the lounge her only

company. After she finished eating, she swilled her bowl out and left it on the draining board. She found Lauren lying on the couch, knees bent, with paperwork resting on her thighs.

"That casserole was wonderful. Thank you very much." Lauren glanced up at her, a soft smile on her lips. "My mother would be proud. That was her recipe. She always cooked it for me when I was sick. It never failed to make me feel better." Her eyes glistened with unshed tears. "God, I miss her."

Vivian reached out and squeezed Lauren's shoulder. "I know how you feel. Not a day goes by I don't think about my dad."

Lauren swung her feet to the floor and sat up. She tossed the paperwork to the side, making room for Vivian to sit at the other end of the sofa. "I had no idea he'd passed."

"Why would you? We've only just met. He was the reason why I began working for your father. They were best friends growing up. Gregory came to the funeral, and we kept in touch over the years. When the job became available, I was the first person Gregory thought of."

Lauren's forehead creased as she narrowed her gaze, her lips pursing. "I guess that's why you're so loyal to him."

"You make it sound like a bad thing. I know you have your issues with your father, but leave me out of them." Vivian stood from the sofa and walked away. Lauren's quiet voice stopped her.

"I'm sorry."

Vivian glanced over her shoulder at her. "I've had enough of being stuck in the middle of you two. I'm in a no-win situation. If I don't spy on you, Gregory will probably fire me. If I do spy on you, any trust that we might be building between us will be gone, and working here will be a nightmare."

"I am sorry, Vivian." Lauren stood and faced her. "You shouldn't be in this position. It's not fair of him to ask you to do this, but he has. Just do what he wants and don't worry about me. As you said, we've only just met. I'm going to head to bed. It's been a long day and I'm tired."

Vivian didn't get the chance to say anything more, as Lauren strode past into her room and closed the door. Vivian blew out a deep breath. *Why is it we can't have one conversation that doesn't end up in an argument?* It was getting tiresome. Perhaps Lauren was right. Perhaps she should just do what Gregory asked and forget about Lauren's feelings altogether. She couldn't do that, though. It was painfully clear how much Lauren missed her mother, and although she said she didn't care what Gregory thought of her, it was obvious she was hurting over the fact he didn't like her. Vivian didn't want to be another person who caused Lauren any hurt. She was back to her original plan. Help Lauren succeed and placate Gregory as much as possible.

Vivian made sure the front door was locked, then switched off all the lights. She had wanted a shower before bed, but now she couldn't be bothered. Her words with Lauren and the casserole bloating her out had exhausted her. She stripped off her clothing and slipped into the cool bedding completely naked, her preferred way of sleeping. She was a nightmare for fidgeting while she tried to fall asleep. Wearing pyjamas only ever managed to tangle her up. Besides, she liked the feel of the sheets against her bare skin. She couldn't shut her thoughts off, though, and it wasn't until the early hours that she finally managed to drift off into an uneasy sleep.

CHAPTER SIX

The next morning, Vivian entered the kitchen to make herself a cup of coffee. She switched on the kettle, then leaned back against the countertop, folding her arms across her chest. She was angry. She had been up since seven o'clock that morning, setting up the computer and laying out her files. As promised, she had logged into Bridger Holdings. She'd checked her email and seen to any pressing matters. What had put her in a foul mood was a late-night email from Gregory. He had sent her a list of things to watch out for with Lauren, things he wanted to be updated about. He expected a report at the end of each day. Vivian couldn't fathom why. She had told him she would let him know if there were any problems, but apparently, that wasn't good enough. He wanted to know about everyone who was working for Lauren, every penny she spent, and what she got up to in her free time. This was a case of more than just trust issues. He was actively wanting to know every detail about Lauren's life. Vivian still couldn't imagine what had caused this distrust between them, and she wanted to know what was going on. It was time to talk to Lauren before they set off for the day.

She finished making her coffee, then went in search of Lauren. She found her in the lounge, staring out the window. Vivian glanced through the glass, seeing a flurry of snow drift down from the grey skies. "That doesn't look good," she said, causing Lauren to start.

"It should be fine. I checked the forecast. The snow should stop within the next hour. It doesn't seem to be settling, so we should be able to get out and drive around town."

"About that." Vivian placed her mug on the fireplace and then sat in the armchair. "I need to talk to you about your father."

Lauren sighed. "I thought we settled that last night. You do as he asks, and we get this project finished as soon as possible."

"You need to see this." Vivian shifted and reached into the back pocket of her jeans. She pulled out a printed copy of the email and handed it to Lauren. "This is a list of things he wants me to do. I'm not comfortable with any of it. And unless you can explain to me why he's doing this, then I can't possibly move forward with the project."

Lauren unfolded the piece of paper and scanned the message, her eyes narrowing the further she read. She looked at Vivian for a moment, then balled up the paper and tossed it into the fire. "He's a piece of work." She turned her back and continued to stare out at the falling snow.

Vivian was silent, hoping stoic Lauren would talk. She didn't, and Vivian sighed. "Lauren, you need to tell me what's going on. Why is he being like this?"

Lauren shook her head. "I can't."

"Why not?"

"I promised my mother I'd never tell anyone. Not even Damien knows."

"Knows what?"

Lauren turned around, tear stains on her cheeks. "When my mother began to get sick, she knew something was wrong. She wanted me to know the truth before she forgot everything. She sat me down and told me the story. I was devastated I had been lied to all those years, but there was nothing I could do about it. Even though I hardly saw Gregory, he was still my father. He still raised me. It all made sense why he distanced himself from me, why he hates me so much."

"Lauren, what are you talking about?"

Lauren sat on the couch. She was gripping her hands together so tightly, her knuckles turned white. "You have to promise me not to tell anyone. I don't want anybody finding out."

Vivian nodded, her stomach in knots. Whatever Lauren was about to say would determine Vivian's future position at Bridger Holdings. "I promise."

"Before I was born, and Damien was about three, Dad's company was taking off. He started to spend all his time at work, leaving Mum to raise Damien. Dad never helped. She was stressed and lonely. She met a guy while out shopping. He helped her carry her bags to the car and they chatted. Mum said he was kind and handsome. They exchanged numbers and became really good friends. Dad didn't know about him. Dad was never there anyway, so didn't see him coming and going from the house." Lauren paused for a moment. "His name was Peter, and he's my biological father." Lauren swiped at her cheeks as more tears dripped from her eyes. "There was no way she could tell my dad I wasn't his. She hid it from him and from Peter. She broke up with Peter, told him she wanted to work things out with Gregory. She told me she never saw him again."

"Oh Lauren, that's terrible."

"It gets worse. I was a happy kid growing up. Damien and I played together, we had lots of friends. We didn't see Dad much, but he still bought us gifts and took us on holiday. Everything was going great, or so we thought. But Mum wanted a divorce. She couldn't stay with him any longer. She wanted us both to go with her to France, but Dad wouldn't allow it. Mum wasn't going to just let him keep us. She told him the truth about my parentage. He hit her, then threw her out. A few days later, he packed me a bag, then dropped me off at the hotel she was staying in. I didn't know what was going on, but I didn't care. I wanted to be with my mum, so I was fine with leaving. We were in France the next day. I didn't see him for five years after that. When I hit sixteen, I took a flight back home to see him. He was my dad and I missed him."

"What did he do when you showed up?"

"I went to his office. He was stunned. He stared at me for a long while, then began to question me on why I was there. I didn't understand why he wouldn't hug me and tell me he missed me. Eventually, he took me to lunch. We talked for a bit and he sent me back to France."

Vivian retrieved her coffee from the fireplace. She took a large gulp, not caring it had gone cold. She sat next to Lauren instead of returning to the armchair. She could only imagine how confused Lauren would have been at that age, not knowing why her father behaved that way. *It makes sense now, why there were no photos of Lauren on Gregory's wall.* She placed her hand on Lauren's knee. "Keep going," she murmured.

"It was the same every time I came back. He never told me he wasn't my dad. I don't think he even knows that I know. Mum told me about Peter five years ago. I never bothered to try and track him down. For all I know, Peter isn't his real name. He could have been married and didn't want Mum to know." She shrugged. "Anyway, as we both know, my father doesn't trust me. My only guess is that he thinks I'm after his money and wants to stop me from getting it."

Vivian shook her head. "I don't understand. He came to my office after we first discussed the business plan with you. He asked me to keep an eye on you. I asked him why he would invest if he didn't trust you and expected you to fail. He said he wants to be a good father. By investing, it would show you he believed in you, even though he didn't. That way, when you failed, he could say he supported you."

"Vivian, what's the one thing I keep telling you?"

Vivian shook her head, furrowing her brows.

"Better the devil you know. He clearly thinks I'm up to something. What better way to find out what that is than by having a ringside seat."

"This is all ridiculous. It seems like a lot of time and effort, and money, just on a hunch. Why not just tell you no?"

"My father is a control freak. He needs to know everything about everything. In his mind, I probably am after his fortune. What he doesn't seem to grasp is I only want to make a life for myself. I've never wanted anything from him, except his love."

Vivian stood and stared out the window at the dwindling snow, much the same way Lauren had. "I'm not sure I can continue with this."

"You have to."

"Why?" Vivian turned around sharply, glaring at Lauren. "What goes on between you two is none of my concern. It'll be best all-round if I just leave here and quit my job. I'm not going to be stuck in the middle of this game you're both playing."

Lauren rose to her feet, her gaze pleading. "You have to stay, Vivian. If you leave, he'll pull the plug on the whole thing, and I'll be left with nothing."

"Again, not my business."

Anger flashed across Lauren's features. "How can you be so cold?"

"How can you expect me to do this? This is going to get ugly. I don't want to spend the next few months reporting on everything you do to a man I'm not sure I like anymore. Why would I?"

"Because I need you. You're the only one who can help me get this off the ground. I'm begging you, please, Vivian. Please don't leave."

Vivian uncrossed her arms, placing her hands on her hips. She lowered her head, closing her eyes. She couldn't bear to see the desperate plight Lauren was in. Her good sense told her to pack her bags and never look back. She made the mistake of looking up and into Lauren's wounded gaze. "You're asking a lot of me. I don't even know you."

"I know."

"If he finds out I know the truth, I can only imagine what he would do."

"I've kept the truth from him for years. He won't find out."

"I could lose my career over this."

Lauren nodded.

"You're asking me to risk everything I've worked for to help someone I've only met a handful of times.

"Yes."

Vivian closed her eyes again for a moment, her heart warring with her head. Was Lauren worth taking the risk for? She's been open and honest with me. Answered every question I've ever asked her. Told me about her mother's affair and her biological father. She's never lied to me. She deserves the chance to start afresh. If lying to Gregory helps her, shouldn't I do it? Her heart won out. She opened her eyes. "Fine, I'll stay. But he must never find out the truth."

Lauren rushed forward, pulling her into a fierce hug. "Thank you so much. You have no idea how much this means to me."

Vivian's arms came around Lauren's waist, holding her tightly. She couldn't stop herself from breathing in her scent. It was just as she remembered all those months ago. She savoured every moment of their bodies fused, knowing it would probably be the last time she would have Lauren in her arms. "Please don't fuck this up."

"I won't, I promise."

She hadn't realised she had spoken the words out loud. What Lauren didn't know was that Vivian meant those words for herself. Vivian stepped back. "I think we should get going. The snow has stopped."

Lauren cleared her throat. "Okay. I'll just grab the plans the architect drew up. I'll meet you at the car."

Vivian shoved her feet into her boots and slipped on her jacket. She purposely left her mobile in her room. She had no doubt Gregory would be calling at some point, and she just didn't want to deal with him yet. She planned on enjoying the day, learning about the job site and the local area. Later, once home, she and Lauren would have to discuss exactly what they would be telling Gregory in her daily report. A task she wasn't looking forward to.

†

"Wow," Vivian said. "Look at that view."

Lauren stepped up beside her, lips pulling into a huge grin as she looked over the fields below. Clouds and fog blocked much of the visage, but what you could see was breathtaking. So far, Lauren had shown Vivian the job site, the local villages, and some of the hotspots around the main town. They'd shared a pleasant few hours, despite the hard conversation that morning. She hadn't planned on telling Vivian everything, but for some reason, Lauren just couldn't say no to her.

The bluff they were standing on was something private to Lauren. She had found the lookout when she'd visited earlier in the year. She wanted to share with Vivian the peace the place always gave her, almost like a thank you for staying. It had been hard to ask her not to leave. It was clear Vivian wanted to. Lauren knew she was putting Vivian in an awful position, but she had to do something to make her stay. This project was her last chance to start anew. She had to make it work. She pulled in a deep breath of the frigid air, pleased the snow hadn't returned.

"When I came here in summer, I climbed to the top of that hill." She pointed to a set of three large, rolling hillsides to the left. She would love to have taken Vivian up there where the view was even better, but in this weather, it wasn't feasible. They would have to walk for a good forty minutes to reach the top. The cold wind would make the journey uncomfortable. Besides, it would be getting dark soon. Lauren didn't fancy being stuck in the middle of nowhere in the dark. "You could see for miles. It was the most beautiful sight I'd seen in a long time."

"I can imagine." Vivian turned to Lauren, her cheeks red from the cold. "You picked a perfect place to open your first health club."

"This part of Scotland is very affluent. The amenities I came up with should entice a lot of people. It helps being near the golf course. One of the ideas is to have the men play a round or two of golf while the women get pampered."

Vivian shook her head, smiling. "You're being very stereotypical."

"It's a stereotype for a reason." Lauren shrugged. "Don't forget, we've also got the gym and pool. The clientele will be mixed, with something for everyone. It's getting colder. Come on." Without thinking, Lauren took Vivian's gloved hand and led the way back to the car. Once settled inside, she started the engine. Vivian's voice stopped her from pulling away.

"Wait. Before we head back, I want to talk to you."

"Didn't we do enough of that this morning?" Lauren wasn't in the mood to go over it all again, but if that was what Vivian wanted, she would. *Why do I keep doing everything she asks?* Deep down, she knew why. She was attracted to Vivian. No surprise there, but she didn't have to make it so easy for Vivian to open her vault of private thoughts. Laying yourself bare was hard for anyone, but Lauren found it especially difficult. She only ever talked openly with her mother. The last five years without Celeste had been awful. Having Vivian near made Lauren want to open up again. Somehow, Vivian put Lauren at ease and Lauren found she didn't mind being honest with her.

"Nope. I wanted to thank you for telling me about what happened. It couldn't have been easy."

Lauren slouched back into her seat, resting her hands loosely on the steering wheel. "I've never told anyone." Lauren had this big secret and no one to share it with. Telling Vivian felt like the load had been lifted.

"Thank you for trusting me. I'm still not comfortable with the whole thing, but I want to help you. We need to discuss what we are going to tell your father. He'll be expecting an update tonight."

"Vivian, just do what he wants." Lauren stole a glance and noticed Vivian's frown. It was clear she wasn't happy about helping Gregory. "I'm not hiding anything. All the people working on the project are on the up and up. I don't plan on going out every night, so there will be no news on that front. I have nothing to hide from him. Despite his lack of faith in me, he's still my dad. Would I have liked to have a proper relationship with him? Of course. But he's not interested in that. He'll eventually see I'm not up to anything and will probably back off and let me get on with it. Once this is over, you'll be able to go back to work, knowing your job is safe and he's happy with what you did."

"I'm not sure I want to go back," Vivian said in a whisper, her gaze fixed in the distance. "And not just because of all this."

"Is it because he has romantic feelings for you?"

Vivian's head whipped around. "You know about that?"

"It's not hard to miss." Lauren grinned. Anyone with eyes could see the way Gregory fawned over her. "Besides, the night of his Christmas party, he told me to keep my filthy hands off you."

"What?"

"Yep. Because I'm gay, I must fancy every woman I meet." *Not every woman, just Vivian.*

"How dare he presume I belong to him."

Lauren stared at Vivian, seeing the anger in her features. It was the same look she wore the night of the spring party. And oh how it had turned her on. Lauren couldn't resist teasing her. "Little does he know it's not my hands he needs to worry about."

"Pardon?"

"You know what I'm talking about."

"No, I don't."

"You don't need to be embarrassed." Lauren hadn't planned on bringing it up. It would be better all-round if they kept on pretending they didn't know each other, but Lauren didn't want that. They were becoming friends, at least she hoped they were, and she didn't want any secrets between them. "I liked it, well, apart from the dressing down. That sucked. But the rest?" She smiled wistfully. "Yeah, it was fun."

"You remember me?" Vivian's cheeks tinted pink again.

"Of course I do. Aside from being humiliated when you called me stupid, reckless, and despicable, I have never been so turned on in my life."

Vivian looked away. "Don't say that."

"Why? It's the truth. You know, I probably have a lot to thank you for."

"How so?"

"If it wasn't for that night, I wouldn't have sorted myself out and decided I wanted to make something of my life. It was your words that made me realise how I was letting myself, and my mother, down. I left that night, disgusted in myself. If not for you, we wouldn't be sitting in this car about to embark on a life-changing project."

"Why did you pretend you didn't know me?"

"It was obvious in Dad's office you were embarrassed about seeing me again. I knew we had met before, but I couldn't remember from where. When you spoke to me after we left, it hit me. You were the woman who had kissed me senseless and was on the verge of making me come."

"Do you have to be so graphic?" Her blush deepened.

"Why? It happened. No point lying about it."

"Are you always so honest?"

"I try to be. If you ask me a question, I'm not going to bullshit you. I'm getting too old for games. Lying just makes things worse."

"You're lying to your father."

Lauren shook her head. *Why does she have to keep bringing him up? I'm trying to tell her I find her attractive and she's thinking of my dad.* "That's not fair. I'm protecting myself. He doesn't think I know he's not my father. Why bring it up when all it will do is cause trouble. I also don't want Damien to be hurt by this."

"That's a lie."

"No. It's not." It was Lauren's turn to stare out the window.

"It is. You don't want Damien to know, because you think you'll lose him as a brother."

"How do you know that?" Vivian's hand covered her own on the steering wheel, the feel of the glove rough against her skin.

"It's true, isn't it?"

"He's all I have left. I don't know how he'll take being lied to all these years. I don't want him resenting me."

"He wouldn't."

"I'm not willing to risk it." She pulled her hand free. "Anyway, we weren't talking about that. I'm not sure why it is I tell you the truth when you ask me something. Even from that first day, I always answered your questions."

"Maybe because you trust me?"

Lauren laughed. "I wouldn't go that far. I'm not a hundred percent sure you won't use what I tell you against me, but I also know that when you look at me this feeling of calm comes over me. Like I've known you for years. Telling you my secrets seems like the right thing to do."

"There you go again with that honesty."

"I can't help it." She shook her head. "I'm sorry."

"Don't apologise. It's nice. I'll just have to make sure that I'm willing to hear the answer to any question I ask."

"Good. Just don't ask me if I want a replay of that night."

"Lauren. You know nothing can happen, don't you?"

"I know nothing of the sort."

"Well, let me make it clear. I'm here to do my job. Nothing more, nothing less."

Lauren put the car in gear and pulled away, glancing at Vivian. "Now who's lying." Lauren had dated enough women in her time to know when someone was interested in her, and Vivian was definitely interested. "There's one more place I want to show you before we call it a day."

CHAPTER SEVEN

"How's it going?" Lauren leaned on Vivian's doorframe and watched her type on the keyboard. The evening had been a quiet affair. They had ordered pizza and taken turns showering. Once they finished eating, Vivian had excused herself to her room to do her work for Gregory. Lauren hadn't seen her in four hours, which was fine, she had her own work to do ready for the big day tomorrow. However, the clock was ticking and soon it would be the new year. She had a surprise for Vivian. She just hoped she'd like it.

"Fine." Vivian swivelled around on her chair to face Lauren, her eyes ringed with grey. "I sent my report off to Gregory. I told him you showed me around and everything was looking good." Lauren waggled her eyebrows. Vivian inhaled deeply, clearly not happy with the flirty gesture. "About the project."

"I'm just teasing."

"Please don't."

"Sorry." Lauren straightened, stuffing her hands into the pockets of her jogging bottoms. "Listen, it's coming up to midnight. I thought you might like to watch the fireworks on TV. There's also some pizza left if you're hungry."

"Okay, thank you. I'll just log off, then I'll be there."

Lauren went back into the living room. She muted the television and dimmed the lights. The fake candles she'd switched on earlier gave the room a romantic feel. She had probably gone overboard, but she wanted to make Vivian not hate being her 'assignment' so much. This was the only thing she could think of. She glanced up at the banners hanging from the walls to make sure they were straight, then filled two glasses with the champagne she had chilled.

"What's all this?"

Lauren watched closely as Vivian scanned the room and walked over to her. "Happy New Year, Vivian." She handed her a glass, hating she had forgotten to bring proper flutes. "My dad told me you had to cancel plans with your sister to come up here, so I thought I'd throw you your own little party."

"Where did you get all this from?" Vivian motioned around the room.

"I, uh, brought it with me."

"You planned this before we left Cornwall?"

Lauren shrugged, still not sure if she had overstepped her boundaries, or whether Vivian liked it or not. Vivian was quiet for a long moment, taking it all in. Lauren's pulse began to flutter wildly. *She hates it. This was a mistake.* She put her glass down, intent on apologising.

"This is so sweet of you," Vivian said quietly.

Lauren grinned. "It's no big deal."

"It is a big deal." Vivian reached out and squeezed her forearm, her gaze boring into Lauren's. "Thank you." Vivian was the first to break eye contact. "How did you know I like champagne?"

"You seem like the classy type."

"Stereotypes again?"

"Just a hunch."

By silent agreement, they sat on the couch. Lauren turned the sound back on the TV, enough to hear the festivities happening in London, but low enough to not disrupt conversation.

"What do you normally do for New Year's?" Vivian asked.

"Not much. I used to go out with friends before Mum got sick." Lauren sipped her drink. "These past few years, I spent them with her in the home."

"This is the first year without her, isn't it?"

"Yes."

"Is that why you wanted to come up here early?"

Lauren nodded. "I didn't fancy sitting in my apartment alone. And no way I would spend New Year's with my father. My brother is with his wife's family. I should apologise to you, though."

Vivian's forehead creased as she raised her brows. "Why?"

"Because I didn't want to be down south, I dragged you away from your family. If not for me, you'd be with the people you love tonight. I'm sorry."

"Lauren, this isn't your fault. You didn't know Gregory would insist I oversee the project."

"No, but when I found out, I should have delayed everything. Again, this isn't fair on you."

Vivian touched Lauren's thigh, her head dipping as she captured Lauren's gaze. "I don't mind, and you've more than made up for it with all this." She motioned around the room.

Lauren got lost in Vivian's gaze, her eyes appearing almost black in the dim light of the room. The candlelight flickered over her face, dancing over her smooth skin. Lauren wet her lips. "The countdown has started."

Ten, nine, eight...

"Happy New Year, Vivian."

Four, three, two...

"Happy New Year, Lauren."

One.

They clinked their glasses. Lauren swallowed hard. "It's tradition to kiss someone at midnight," she murmured, shifting ever so closer to Vivian. All she wanted at this moment was to taste her lips again, to see if they were as soft as she remembered.

"Are you joking?"

"No." Lauren shook her head imperceptibly. "Your choice."

Vivian gazed at her for what seemed like hours. The sound of *Auld Lang Syne* sang from the TV. She glanced down to Lauren's lips, only inches away, then back up into Lauren's eyes. "Well, it is tradition."

Lauren nodded. "It is."

Lauren wasn't sure who moved first, it didn't matter. All she could feel was Vivian's lips on hers, her tongue seeking entry. Her memories of the first kiss paled in comparison. *Maybe because I'm sober.* Lauren's hand found its way into Vivian's hair, clutching her tightly. The sound of her glass hitting the floor didn't stop the kiss. Her need for Vivian overrode all else. She never thought she could feel this strongly for someone she hardly knew, but she did. She wanted her. Now.

Vivian pushed at Lauren's chest, her breathing laboured. "Okay. That's enough." She swiped her hand across her mouth and got to her feet. "I have to get to bed. Goodnight, Lauren." She handed Lauren her glass and strode from the room.

"Goodnight," Lauren whispered into the empty room, closing her eyes. "What are you doing? You idiot." She hadn't meant for it to go so far. All she'd wanted was a little kiss, not a full-on make-out session. *At least this time Vivian kept her hands to herself, unfortunately.*

Lauren had messed up. Vivian had said she hadn't wanted anything to happen between them, but Lauren just had to push her. *She could have said no. She didn't have to kiss me back.* She stood from the couch and switched off the television, then pulled down the banners and put the candles away. What had started as a nice gesture had turned into a disaster. Vivian had run away from her, clearly mortified at what they had done. Shame washed over Lauren. She wasn't looking forward to facing her in the morning. *I'll just have to make sure I'm gone before she wakes up.*

†

Vivian was startled awake when she heard the front door slam, her heart racing. The faint rumble of a car engine sounded through the darkened room. She glanced at her phone, not quite six o'clock. It was clear Lauren had left early to avoid seeing her. *I can't believe I kissed her, after everything I said.* Lauren had been so kind as to give her a mini New Year's Eve party, and Vivian allowed her heart to rule over her head. Sitting on the sofa, so close to each other, had been intoxicating. She couldn't do anything *but* kiss her. She knew that if she'd continued kissing Lauren, they would have ended up in bed together. That was something Vivian wasn't going to do. They needed to talk, to clear the air. They had to put their attraction aside for the sake of the project.

With that goal in mind, Vivian got ready for the day. There was no point staying in bed now she was awake. After breakfast, she switched on the computer and set about logging into Bridger Holdings. Hopefully, a day of looking at numbers would help erase the feel of Lauren's lips from her mind.

The day wore on, and by ten o'clock that night, there was still no sign of Lauren. Vivian had tried calling her, but she never answered. She could have driven to the job site, but this was a conversation they needed to have in private. She settled under the covers, her ears straining through the dark. An hour later, the front door opened. The sound of boots hitting the floor clued Vivian into it being Lauren coming home and not a murderer. The shower came on, then off, followed by the sound of Lauren's bedroom door closing.

Vivian was tempted to cross the hallway and demand answers, but she was too weary for a confrontation this late at night. She closed her eyes and drifted off, determined to be up before Lauren the next day.

Her wish didn't come true. Vivian again was awoken by the closing of the front door. She checked her phone. Five forty-five. This pattern went on for two more days, when Vivian had enough. She was angry that Lauren was acting childish. Not only that, Vivian had no idea was what was happening at the job site. Her reports to Gregory were sparse. She could tell from his responses he wanted more information. It was time to track Lauren down and demand to see her.

An hour later, Vivian parked her car by the entrance. A huge security guard stood by the main opening to the closed-off site. She stepped from the car and approached, straining her head back to look him in the eye.

"Where's Lauren Bridger?" she asked, her voice filled with annoyance.

The security guard glanced at her, then jerked his head behind him. "Somewhere on the site. Who are you?" He crossed his arms over his massive chest.

"I'm a friend, and also the accounts manager. Point me in her direction, please." She tried to step around him, but his hand on her bicep stopped her progress.

"Ma'am, you can't go in there without a hardhat."

"Then please get me one."

He looked down at her feet. "You don't exactly have the right footwear, either."

She glanced down, rolling her eyes at the heels she wore. She couldn't go traipsing through all the mud in these. "Fine. Call her and tell her to come out and see me."

He was quiet for a moment, eyeing her with pursed lips, then reached for his phone. "Boss? There's a lady here, wants to see you…Shorter than you, angry looking… Boss? Okay." He clipped his phone back onto his belt. "She'll be right with you."

"Thank you." Vivian went back to the car and leaned against the passenger door. Her wool coat did nothing to stop the cold penetrating through to her skin. A full five minutes passed before Lauren approached, not looking very happy.

"Vivian, what are you doing here?"

Vivian glanced at Lauren's cheek, a two-inch cut ran perpendicular to her jawline. "You've hurt yourself."

"What?" Lauren frowned.

"Your cheek, it's bleeding."

"It's nothing. What do you want?"

"In case you've forgotten, I'm supposed to be a part of this project. That means I need to know what's going on, daily." She tried to keep her voice calm, but it was tinged with irritation.

Lauren blinked at her. "That's why you're here?"

"Not the only reason, but you're avoiding me."

"I didn't think you'd want to see me after the other night." Before Lauren looked away, Vivian thought she looked sad.

"Lauren, we're two grown-ups. We need to talk about this. If you keep shutting me out, Gregory will be up here trying to find out why my reports are nothing but filler."

81

Lauren's gaze cut back to her, hard beneath furrowed brows. "That's your only concern, for him?"

Vivian took a step forward and briefly touched Lauren's shoulder, needing the contact. She hadn't seen her in four days. She hadn't realised how much she missed her. "I'm concerned about you, us." She dropped her hand. "Please be home at a reasonable hour."

"I'll try."

"Not try. Be home early."

Lauren looked to the ground. She nodded, then walked away.

"And take care of that cut," Vivian called after her.

She got back into her car and headed home, praying Lauren wouldn't let her down. If she did, then Vivian would have no choice but to pack up and leave. If Gregory pulled the plug on the project, that would be Lauren's fault for being childish.

†

Vivian sat on a stool next to the kitchen island. She drummed her fingers on the wooden surface, while she sipped the wine in her other hand. Her gaze kept finding the clock. Eight in the evening. She had expected Lauren home ages ago. She was about to pick up her mobile to call her, when the front door opened. She heard the boots drop to the floor. Lauren briefly appeared in the kitchen archway. Her face was flushed, probably from being out in the cold all day. The cut on her cheek had dried, but it was clear Lauren hadn't attempted to clean it up. Her hair was wild, her jeans and jacket caked in mud and dirt. Vivian crossed one leg over the other, clenching her centre. Lauren was the single most gorgeous woman Vivian had ever seen, even covered in grime.

"I'm just going to take a shower," Lauren said, her gaze glued to the tiled floor. She walked on, not giving Vivian a chance to respond.

Vivian sighed and took another a sip. She waited patiently while Lauren showered, thinking about what she wanted to say to her. A few minutes later, Lauren came back into the kitchen and sat opposite Vivian, folding her hands on the island.

"There's wine if you want it." Vivian pushed the bottle closer to Lauren.

"I'm fine."

"You're bleeding again." The shower had loosened the scab, and a small trickle of blood snaked its way down Lauren's neck. "Why didn't you put anything on it like I said?"

"I forgot."

"Hang on." Vivian stood, tightening her silk robe, and went to the bathroom. The scent of Lauren's shampoo still lingered in the air, causing Vivian to inhale deeply. She opened the cabinet and retrieved the first aid kit. She went back into the kitchen and grasped Lauren's shoulder, encouraging her to swivel on the stool to face her. Lauren opened her thighs, allowing Vivian to step in closer. Lauren still hadn't looked her in the eye, her gaze downcast. "Right, hold still." Vivian cleaned the wound and taped a small dressing to the area. It wasn't a deep cut, so wouldn't need stitches.

"Why are you being nice to me?"

"I'm not. I just don't want the landlady pissed because there are bloodstains on the tile."

Lauren frowned. "Oh."

"I'm kidding." Vivian cupped Lauren's uninjured cheek, tilting her head up. "Lauren, I care about you. There's no denying that I'm attracted to you."

"Then what's the problem? Is it because of my dad?"

"Partly." Vivian stepped away from Lauren's yearning expression. She threw out the detritus and washed her hands, then retook her seat on her stool. "There are things you don't know, things I promised to never do again."

"Tell me."

Vivian shook her head. "No." There were some things she never wanted to think about again, let alone talk about.

"Why not? I've told you some really big stuff. Why can't you be honest with me?"

"I've always been a private person. Even as a child. It's not easy for me to open up. We can't all be free and easy with things."

Lauren furrowed her brow. "You make it sound like that's a bad thing."

"The more people know about you, the more ammunition they have to destroy you."

Anger flashed across Lauren's features. "I'm not like that." She reached over the island, grasping Vivian's hand where it rested next to her glass. "I'd never do anything to hurt you."

"You don't even know me."

"Then tell me something about yourself." Lauren looked away for a moment. "What did you do before working for my father?"

"Not exactly an easy question to start with."

"I'm listening."

Vivian stared at Lauren, warring within herself whether to talk about one of the most painful experiences she'd ever had. Lauren didn't flinch under her scrutiny. *She's right, she has told me some pretty big secrets. It wouldn't hurt to give a little back. Perhaps then she might forget all about this attraction we have for each other.* "I'm not proud of this," she warned, then took a deep breath. "I had an affair with my boss. She told me she was getting a divorce. She wouldn't stop flirting with me. Eventually, I gave in. Three years later, I found out she was still happily married. I confronted her. She didn't deny it, so I told her I wanted to stop seeing her."

"I assume she didn't take that very well?"

"No. She said if I stopped the affair, she'd fire me. I quit there and then and haven't seen her since. Gregory called about a month later and offered me a job. I swore, after Lesley, I'd never get involved with someone I work with again." There was more to the story, like the heartache she suffered. She'd truly thought Lesley was in love with her. The betrayal of knowing she had been lied to, and the humiliation of Lesley watching her pack up her desk, had been devastating. Vivian swore off relationships after that. Meeting Lauren let her know that she wanted to find someone again. It just couldn't be Lauren. It would be too messy.

"We don't work together, not really."

"But I work for Bridger Holdings." Vivian waved her hand in the air. "Same difference."

"No. In a few months, we'll have no reason to work together again. You can do what you want then."

I can barely stop myself from begging to have you now, a few months of this would be torture. "The problem is, Lauren, I don't think I'll be able to stay away from you for that long." Vivian glanced down at Lauren's mouth, memories of their kisses suffusing her body with heat. "Every time you look at me, I just want to kiss you."

Lauren rose from the stool. She came around to stand next to Vivian, her face inches away. She cupped Vivian's cheek. "Then kiss me."

Vivian swallowed hard, her resolve weakening. She shook her head, pushing Lauren back. She stood and went to the sink, her back to Lauren. "I can't."

"I won't hurt you, Viv."

"I believe you." Vivian turned around, folding her arms across her chest, feeling her nipples harden against the fabric of the dressing gown. "But no, we can't do this."

"So, what, we just forget we're insanely attracted to one another?"

"I couldn't even if I wanted to," she muttered. "You're very hard to resist."

"Well, we can't avoid each other. To use your words, Gregory wants more than filler in your reports."

Vivian shrugged. "I guess we come up with a schedule. When you get home every night, you tell me what happened that day, and I'll make my report. If you need funds, you can text or email me."

"Do you know what? I think I'll take Thomas up on staying at his. It'll be easier all-around if I'm not here." Lauren turned on her heel and walked away. Vivian followed her down the hallway.

"You don't have to leave. We can make this work."

Lauren spun around, causing Vivian to bump into her. "Do you really think I can come home every night, catch you up on the events on the day, then go sleep in my room when I know you're just across the hall? It'll be agony."

Vivian looked at the carpet, hating how hurt Lauren sounded. "It's not easy for me, either."

"But it's your game, and you make the rules. As long as I do what you and Gregory want, everything is great. I'm tired of just being a player in my life that can be moved around at will." Lauren went into her room and pulled her suitcase out from under the bed. She tossed it onto the mattress and yanked the zipper open.

"It's not like that."

"Really? Cuz it feels that way to me." Lauren straightened, her eyes flashing. "All I have ever done is try to be his daughter, but he doesn't want me. And you don't want me either. Nobody wants me." She threw her hands in the air. "The only person who did is dead, and I'm alone. Do you have any idea how hard it is to be constantly pushed away? To be lied to and spied on. I was willing to let you follow me around just so he'd stay off my back. And I was fine with that because it meant I got to see you every day." She softened her features. "You have no idea what you do to me."

"Yes, I do."

"No, you don't."

"I do, because you do the same to me." Vivian stepped forward and grabbed Lauren's hand. She brought it through the opening of her robe, pressing her fingers into her underwear. "Feel me." She closed her eyes, as Lauren's hand pushed harder against her.

"Vivian," Lauren whispered, her voice shaking.

Vivian opened her eyes, seeing the want in Lauren's gaze. "I've been like this since the moment you walked in, so don't try and tell me I don't know how you feel because I do." She stepped back, Lauren's hand dropping away. She quickly re-tied the sash and marched across to her room, her face burning hot, her pulse thrumming in her ears. *I can't believe I just did that!*

"Vivian, wait. You can't just do that and walk away."

Vivian turned, seeing a frustrated Lauren in her doorway. "I don't know what to do."

"Yes, you do." Lauren came fully into the room, taking Vivian in her arms and running her hands up her back. "I'm here, all you have to do is say yes."

"This is a mistake." Vivian gazed up at Lauren, her legs trembling. "I shouldn't have agreed to stay."

"Why did you?"

Vivian reached up and cupped Lauren's cheeks, smiling softly. "Because of you, Lauren. Because of you." Tears sprang from her eyes, Lauren pulled her into a tight hug.

"Shh, it's okay."

"No, it's not."

"Vivian, look at me." Vivian lifted her head from Lauren's chest. "Everything is okay."

"How can you say that? I have no idea what I'm doing anymore."

"We don't need to figure it out tonight. We've got time."

Vivian shook her head. All the time in the world wouldn't change what she wanted. She wanted Lauren, and she was done making excuses and running from this. She was tired of trying to do the right thing. From the moment she'd laid eyes on Lauren, she was drawn to her. This was more than likely going to be a cluster fuck, but she didn't care. It was time to do what she wanted for a change.

"I don't want to wait any longer. You've been in my head for months." She took Lauren's hand and pulled her to the edge of the bed. She untied the sash, giving Lauren a glimpse of her bare chest. Had this been her plan all along? To seduce Lauren. She had said she had wanted to talk about the project, but why dress in only a silk robe and underwear? It didn't matter. What mattered was having Lauren inside of her, and now.

"Make love to me, Lauren."

Lauren's gaze bored into Vivian's, her hands balled into fists, as if stopping herself from reaching out. "Are you sure?"

"Yes."

"What about my dad?"

"I don't want to think about him right now. All I want is your hands and mouth on me."

CHAPTER EIGHT

Vivian held her breath as Lauren stepped forward, bringing her within touching distance. Lauren's hands swept up Vivian's arms, across her collarbones, and onto her chest. Her fingers brushed the robe aside and off her shoulders, while her mouth found Vivian's neck. Vivian tilted her head back, as Lauren's lips trailed kisses over her skin, then finally latched onto her aching nipple.

"God, Lauren. That feels so good." Vivian threaded her hands into Lauren's hair, holding her tight against her.

"You taste good, too." Lauren straightened and took Vivian in a fierce kiss, her hands grabbing hold of her butt. "I can't believe I finally get to have you."

"I've wanted this for so long." Vivian tugged at the hem of Lauren's T-shirt, then pulled it over her head. Her gaze was instantly drawn to Lauren's bare chest, her breasts smooth and pert. They weren't overly big, but they matched her lean form. A flash of colour caught her attention. "You have a tattoo?"

"Yes. In honour of my mother." Lauren leaned in for another kiss, but Vivian stopped her with a hand on her stomach.

"Let me look." Vivian dropped to her knees, her hands clasping the backs of Lauren's thighs. The tattoo was on her right side, a couple of inches below her breast. The design was a silhouette of a mother holding the hand of a little girl. An array of bright colours swirled around behind them, making their silhouette stand out. She glanced up at Lauren. "It's beautiful."

"Not as beautiful as you." Lauren traced her fingers delicately over Vivian's forehead and cheek.

"That was corny." Vivian smiled. She hooked her fingers into the waistband of Lauren's joggers, pulling them down. The scent of her arousal was intoxicating. She stood and took Lauren's hand. "Come lie with me." She lay back on the bed. Lauren slid Vivian's underwear off and tossed the garment aside then settled herself above her, knees either side of Vivian's thighs, before stretching out on top of her. Their lips found each other again. Vivian wrapped her arms around and held tight, as Lauren rocked her hips against hers. Lauren's fingers glided down Vivian's side, the touch bringing chill bumps to her skin even though she was burning hot. "Go inside me."

Lauren locked gazes with her, as her hand moved between them. She slipped inside, and Vivian groaned at the feel of her, reaching depths no one had reached before. Vivian leaned up, kissing Lauren hard. Lauren began to pump her hips, forcing her fingers deeper still. Vivian matched her thrusts. All too soon, Vivian felt her climax building. She wanted it to last longer, to savour this feeling for eternity, but she couldn't. She clutched Lauren to her chest as her walls tightened and released, seemingly pulling Lauren impossibly farther in. Vivian came with a cry. Lauren covered her mouth with her own, swallowing Vivian's passion. Together, they rode out the orgasm. Vivian's body trembled as her heart rate slowed.

"That was incredible," Vivian said, her breathing ragged. She reached up and cupped Lauren's face, her skin coated in sweat. "You're incredible."

Lauren grinned. "Now who's being corny?"

Vivian laughed, then turned serious. "I want my mouth on you. But I don't think I can move." Lauren's grin grew wider.

"You can stay right there." Lauren got to her knees and shifted up over Vivian's head. "Does this work for you?"

"Oh yeah." Vivian gazed up at Lauren, her mouth watering at the sight. She reached both hands up and grabbed Lauren's hips, pulling her down to her hungry lips. The first swipe of her tongue made Lauren flinch. Vivian spent the next few minutes loving every intimate part of Lauren's centre. She was in heaven, and by the sounds of it, so was Lauren. Soon, Lauren began to grind, Vivian kept pace. Her face became wet, and she knew it wouldn't be long before Lauren came. When she did, it was magnificent. Lauren collapsed beside her, her chest rising and falling rapidly as she tried to catch her breath. Vivian rolled onto her side, hooking one leg over Lauren's thigh, her hand on her breast.

"I can't believe we just did that," Lauren said.

A moment of panic suffused Vivian, thinking Lauren thought this was a mistake. She needn't have worried. Lauren rolled her head to the side with a satisfied look on her face.

"I hope you've eaten, as I plan to keep you here all night."

"I had a sandwich. My cooking skills aren't as good as yours."

"My mother taught me well." Lauren shifted so she could face Vivian fully, her fingers roaming over Vivian's side. "Are you okay with this?"

Vivian raised her brows. "Why wouldn't I be?"

"You've spent a lot of time telling me this shouldn't happen. I don't want you to be upset."

Vivian leaned in, giving her a chaste kiss. "Don't worry. If I didn't want to do this, I wouldn't have said yes."

"What do we do now?"

"Well, I plan on exploring every inch of your body. After that, we sleep."

"And tomorrow?"

"Tomorrow is a long way off. Let's just enjoy tonight."

"Okay."

Lauren leaned in and kissed her, rolling Vivian onto her back. They made love again, and again, well into the night and early hours. They finally settled into an exhausted sleep, Vivian cradled in the safety of Lauren's arms.

†

A loud buzzing brought Lauren out of her deep sleep. She opened her eyes, Vivian's dark hair inches from her face. Lauren's arm was wrapped around her waist, Vivian's butt nestled in her pelvis. She smiled as she recalled the night's events. She had come home expecting Vivian to chew her ass off for avoiding her. When she had walked in and seen Vivian sitting on the stool, the blue, silk robe cascading over her body, Lauren had nearly come on the spot. She had rushed into the shower. Setting the water as cold as she could stand, but it didn't help diminish her hunger. When Vivian had finally said she wanted to make love, Lauren had to control her lust. She didn't want to come across as a wild animal, but that's how she felt. She wanted to pin Vivian down and ravish her. She took a deep breath, inhaling Vivian's scent. Their lovemaking was more than sex. It was tender and honest, raw with emotion. There were times Lauren nearly cried with the exquisiteness of it all. *Lying here with Vivian in my arms feels like heaven.*

The buzzing started again, and she realised it was Vivian's phone. She moved the hand that was on Vivian's stomach and gently stroked her bicep. "Viv, your phone is ringing." Vivian mumbled something but didn't wake up. Lauren spoke again. "Come on, get up. It might be important."

"Fine." Vivian lifted her head and picked up the phone from the nightstand. In an instant, she was sitting on the edge of the bed, her bare back to Lauren. "It's your father."

Lauren sighed and flung her arm over her face. He was the last person she wanted to think about. She wanted Vivian again.

"Good morning, Gregory," Vivian said, sounding wide awake. "I'm fine... No, there was a problem with the internet... No, it's all sorted now... I think she's left already... No you don't need to come up here. Everything is fine... Yes, talk to you later."

Lauren removed her arm and looked up at Vivian. Vivian's expression worried her. "Problem?"

Vivian lifted the bedsheet and covered herself, her skin flushing. "I didn't send in his report last night. He thought something might have happened."

"Like what? I murdered you in your sleep?" Lauren couldn't keep the anger from her voice. "What was he gonna do, come in and save you?"

"Lauren, you don't have to be so mad."

"Don't I?" She got out of bed, not caring she was naked, after all, Vivian had touched every part of her last night. There was no point in being shy now. "We had one fucking night," she shouted, pacing the room. "One night just for us, and he's already tainting it."

"Lauren, calm down. He hasn't ruined anything. He was just worried, that's all."

"And now you're defending him." Lauren looked around, spotting her joggers on the floor. She shoved her legs in angrily, then put her T-shirt on. "Perhaps this was a mistake. I'm sorry, Vivian, but I can't compete with him. No matter what I try, he always wins."

Vivian rose from the bed, keeping the sheet wrapped around her. Lauren could see her cheeks twitching from where she was grinding her teeth. "Stop it," Vivian shouted. She went over to Lauren, poking her in the chest. "This isn't a competition, and I'm not a prize to be won. He's still my boss. I wasn't about to tell him I had just spent the night screwing his daughter, and that it was the best night of my life."

Lauren's eyes went wide, her mouth hanging open at Vivian's words. All her anger left her at that moment. She grinned widely. "Best night of your life, hey?"

Vivian blushed but didn't look away. "Yes, it was. And I won't have you ruining the morning after by being angry at me."

Lauren's grin left her face. Her knee-jerk reaction to her father was always anger. She hadn't meant to take it out on Vivian. "I'm sorry."

"I know." Vivian took Lauren's hand and drew her to the bed. They sat side by side. "Lauren, this whole thing is complicated, but our plan doesn't need to change. You keep working, and I'll keep sending in the reports. He won't find anything to complain about, and everything will be fine."

"What about us?"

Vivian looked away for a moment. "We're a separate issue. I didn't plan for this to happen. I tried to keep my feelings in check. But we've crossed that line now."

"And?"

"And I don't want to go back. I don't know what this will lead to, but I enjoy being with you. I'd like to keep seeing you."

"As long as my dad doesn't find out." It was the reality of the situation. Lauren knew deep in her heart that if Gregory ever found out, Vivian would run for the hills.

That's presuming this isn't a short term thing for her. She might just want a winter fling. The thought was depressing. In all her life, Lauren had never found someone as enthralling as Vivian. She wanted to get to know her better, find out about her life, the things she liked, the things she didn't. She wanted to be by her side for as long as possible. If Gregory ever found out, Vivian would be gone.

"I don't know what will happen in the future. All I can tell you is, right now, I can't get enough of you."

Lauren smiled, cupping Vivian's cheek. "I guess that will do, for now." She moved forward and touched her lips to Vivian's, her hand trailing down her neck and settling on her breast. They made love again, but all the while thoughts churned in the back of Lauren's mind. If these few months would be all she would get, she was determined to make the most of them.

CHAPTER NINE

"Hey," Lauren said to Vivian, as she walked in the lounge later that evening. "This looks cosy."

Vivian smiled, seeming pleased with the scene she had set. Thick blankets, piled on the floor, offered an invitation to enjoy the blazing fire. Only the fire's orange glow lit the room. A bottle of wine and two glasses sat on the hearth, and soft music emanated from the radio. All in all, it was very romantic. Lauren had never had anyone do this for her before, and it brought thick emotions to her chest. Vivian wore her silk robe, her damp hair trailing down the back. The scent of lavender bath salts lingered in the air. Lauren's gaze travelled down her body, seeing Vivian's naked form in her mind's eye. She couldn't wait to have her again.

Vivian reached out and took Lauren's hand, leaning in for a quick kiss. Lauren had feared that going to the work site and leaving Vivian on her own all day would douse the flames of passion they had shared that morning. Vivian's hands and mouth were proving that wasn't the case.

"I've got a takeaway keeping warm in the oven," Vivian said, her eyes liquid gold from the firelight. "If you have a quick shower now, I was hoping we could snuggle on the blankets and get to know each other better."

Lauren grinned, squeezing Vivian's ass. "I thought we already did that last night and this morning."

"You know what I mean." Vivian glanced away for a moment, pulling her lower lip between her teeth.

"What is it?" Lauren asked, tilting Vivian's head back so she could look her in the eye.

"It's no secret we're attracted to each other, physically. I could hardly move from my desk all day because my thighs were burning."

"But?"

"I don't want that to be all there is between us. I'm too old for flings. I'm not saying we should be exclusive or anything. I wouldn't want you to feel beholden to me, but I want to get to know you on a deeper level."

"It's clear you don't know me very well. I'm not some party girl who sleeps with anyone I can." Lauren held Vivian tighter as she tried to pull away. "I won't lie to you. I did do that in the past, but there has been no one since the night of the spring party. The night I met you, everything changed...in here." She tapped her chest, above her heart. She shook her head. "I don't know why, but there is something about you that has captured me and won't let go. I would love nothing better than to share a meal with you, have some wine, and lie with you in my arms while we talk." She dipped her head, kissing Vivian's forehead. "Maybe after that, we can do the other thing."

Vivian laughed. "I think that can be arranged." She stepped back. "Go shower while I plate up the food. I hope you like Chinese."

"Love it."

"Good. Don't be long."

Lauren rushed through her shower, and after enjoying the takeaway at the kitchen island, she found herself wearing only her sleep shorts and sports bra, reclining on the blankets with Vivian curled around her. Neither had spoken in the last twenty minutes, and as much as she wanted to know more about Vivian, Lauren was content to just hold her. She closed her eyes as she listened to the radio, thoughts of the future swirling through her mind. *I think she could be the one. I can see us together, doing normal things, like shopping and cooking, for the rest of my life. Is that what she wants?* Although Vivian had said she wasn't into flings, that didn't mean she was after a forever with Lauren. *And let's not forget about my dad. How long before he finds out?* Because he *would* find out. If they carried on seeing each other once they got back to Cornwall, it would only be a matter of time before he was aware of what they were doing.

"You just tensed up." Vivian lifted her head from Lauren's chest. "What's the matter?"

"Nothing. Just thinking."

"About?"

"It doesn't matter. I can't change the future, so no point worrying."

Vivian narrowed her gaze and sighed. She sat up fully, her robe gaping open and revealing her cleavage. "You're thinking about Gregory, aren't you?"

Lauren looked away and considered lying. When she gazed back at Vivian, the lie wouldn't come. "Yes."

"Can't we just enjoy these few months?"

"Of course we can, and we will, but I don't think you seem to understand that when you go back home, I'm still going to want to see you."

"And you're worried I won't want that because of your father finding out?"

Lauren nodded.

"I'm worried about that, too."

"Well, that sucks."

Vivian smiled, then feathered Lauren's hair through her fingers. "Lauren, we both know this is a tricky situation. We've only just begun this. Let's not worry about something that might not happen."

"Are you saying you might get sick of me before then?"

"I was thinking of the other way around." Vivian reached over Lauren and snagged her wine glass, taking a huge sip. She offered the glass to Lauren, who finished it off. Vivian replaced the glass, then settled back against her. "All I know is, I like you and want to stay here, like this, with you, for as long as possible."

"Good enough for me." It wasn't really, but this wasn't the time to be declaring feelings of love. Lauren had no doubt that was where it was heading for her. The spark of intrigue had been lit the night of the spring party, and every meeting since then only compounded Lauren's interest. The spark had turned into a roaring fire that she didn't want to extinguish. She wanted the flames to engulf her, swallow her whole. Vivian was everything she was looking for in a partner. She just hoped Vivian felt the same way about her. *Nothing like being delusional.*

"Tell me about your childhood," Lauren said.

"That's a random topic change."

"I know, but I don't want to think about when our time is up."

"Lauren—"

"Brothers, sisters?"

Vivian sighed, glancing away. "I have a sister. As you know, I was meant to go there for New Year's. She's younger than me. Married to a wonderful guy, and they have three beautiful children. My mum has lived with them since my dad died. My childhood was normal. I fought with my sister a lot, but after we grew up, we became best friends. I did well in school, fell in love with numbers, and led a pretty boring life."

"I doubt it was boring."

"Yep, normal and boring."

Lauren tried to think of something else to ask, but all she could concentrate on was Vivian's hand stroking her bare belly, ever so gently, and getting nearer to her shorts. She trapped Vivian's fingers just as they reached her waistband. "Tell me about when you first realised you liked women."

"I never really thought about it. It was just always that way. I remember when I was nine, we lived opposite friends of my parents. Their daughter was in her early twenties. I remember thinking she was so cool. She had long, curly blonde hair. When she smiled, I couldn't help but smile back. I'd blush profusely whenever she spoke to me. I didn't know what I was feeling, but when I reacted the same way to a friend in high school, I kinda figured it out. How about you?"

"Same, really, just always knew. I told my mum. She was fine with it. Even tried to set me up a few times. Dad didn't take it so well. He couldn't understand it at all. We never speak of it."

Vivian raised her head, gazing down at Lauren. "You either sound sad or angry whenever you talk about him. Were you ever happy growing up with him?"

"I told you before, I was happy as a kid, even when I went to France with Mum. Obviously, I wasn't happy about the divorce, and I missed Damien, but I just got on with things. I wouldn't ever say I was unhappy, but I missed out on Dad's love and support. I just couldn't understand why he was distant with me all those times I visited." Lauren could see the sadness in Vivian's gaze, hating that Vivian felt bad for her. She reached up and cupped her cheek. "It's okay. I'm a grown woman, too old to be seeking my father's approval."

"You say that, but that's not true. If it didn't bother you, you wouldn't be angry all the time."

Lauren dropped her hand, sighing as she did so. "You're right, it does bother me. I would like a normal relationship with him, but it's not going to happen. All I can do now is look to the future." She tried hard not to let her feelings for Vivian show through, but it didn't work. Vivian smiled softly, then leaned down and kissed her, moving over her and straddling her waist.

"To the future," Vivian whispered, kissing her again.

Lauren gave herself over to the kiss, pouring everything she had into enjoying these moments with Vivian. Only time

103

would tell if they would have these moments again after the project was finished.

†

Lauren opened her eyes, the sound of clacking rousing her from slumber. She turned her head to the side and saw Vivian sitting at her makeshift desk. Her back was to Lauren, so Vivian didn't know she was awake. Lauren had no idea of the time. It had to be late. They had made love in the lounge and only made it to bed after eleven o'clock. She still couldn't believe they were lovers. It had happened all so quickly. Lauren had thought these months, stuck in the cottage together, would be horrible, trying to hide her lust for Vivian. She hadn't counted on Vivian feeling the same way.

She threw the covers aside and padded barefoot over to the desk. She wrapped her arms around Vivian from behind. Vivian jumped, her head knocking into Lauren's chin. "Ow." Lauren stepped back, rubbing her face.

"Sorry," Vivian said. "I wasn't expecting you to creep up behind me."

"I didn't exactly creep." Lauren looked over Vivian's shoulder at the computer monitor. "What's got you up so late?"

Vivian looked down at her lap, her hands tightening into fists. "I needed to send Gregory the report."

"Oh, okay." Lauren reached down and grabbed Vivian's robe, slipping her arms in and tying the sash. "I'll leave you to it. I'm a bit hungry anyway. Do you want a sandwich?" Vivian shook her head. "Okay. Won't be long." She turned and headed out into the hallway, her stomach in knots as she entered the kitchen. She had just opened the fridge when she heard Vivian behind her. Lauren closed the door and glanced over her shoulder. "Change your mind about something to eat?"

"No." Vivian leaned against the doorframe, folding her arms across her chest. It was hard to see her features clearly in the dim moonlight. "Are you okay?"

"Of course." Lauren opened a cabinet and retrieved the bread, pulling out two slices.

"You said you were fine with me doing the reports for Gregory."

Lauren glanced up. "And I am." She opened the fridge again and pulled the cheese out, along with the sweet pickle.

"Lauren."

"What?"

Vivian sighed, shaking her head. She pushed off the doorframe and slowly walked over to her. "It must be difficult for you to know I'm doing this."

"You mean because the woman I'm sleeping with is detailing my life to the father who hates me? Why would it be difficult?"

"Damn it, Lauren." Vivian reached out, taking the pickle jar out of Lauren's hands. She slammed it onto the island. "Talk to me."

"We've been over this. I told you I agreed with you doing it. Don't forget it was my idea that you continue to do as he asks."

"But that was before we got involved."

Lauren picked the jar back up, twisting off the lid. "Okay, fine. Yes, I don't like it. It upsets me, but if that's what you need to do to stay here, then I'll put up with it."

She slapped the pickle onto the cheese and squashed the other slice of bread on top, pickle squirting out of the sides. "That doesn't mean I want to sit in the room with you and watch while you do it." She brushed past Vivian into the lounge and settled on the couch. Vivian followed her in. "Just forget about it, okay?"

Vivian dropped to her knees in front of her, taking the plate from her hands and replacing it with her own hands. "I can't forget it. If you're upset, then I'm upset. I don't want you to hurt anymore."

Lauren gazed at Vivian, her heart breaking at the turmoil she was in. She had promised Vivian it would okay to carry on spying on her to appease her father. That should have been the end of it. But it was all different now they were in a relationship, such as it was. She idly thought about pulling the plug on the project. That would put an end to Gregory getting in the way. That wasn't what she wanted. She needed to succeed in her plan so she could finally be free. It wasn't fair to keep putting Vivian in the middle. She closed her eyes, drawing in a deep breath.

"I'm sorry. I promise I'm okay. It was just a shock seeing you actually doing the report. It felt like you were sleeping with me for information."

Vivian shot to her feet, her rage unmistakable. "You think I'm prostituting myself out to you to get information for your father? You think I'm that shallow?"

Lauren stood, reaching out to Vivian, but Vivian stepped away. "It was just a split-second thought. I don't think that." Vivian turned her back on her. "Please, you have to believe me. I would never think that. Sometimes my mouth runs away from me."

"But you did think that, even if it was for just a second. I can't believe this." Vivian spun around. "I can't believe you would sully the time we spent together by thinking I would do that to you, and myself."

"I'm sorry."

"Not good enough. You've made me feel like shit." She stepped around Lauren. "I'm going to bed. You're not welcome in my room tonight."

Lauren watched her leave, then heard the slamming of the bedroom door. She slumped back into the sofa, tears falling from her eyes. *Why would I say that? That's not how I really feel.* Maybe, on some level, Lauren had sabotaged their budding romance to protect herself. She had always been guarded. Her father's distrust of her had always made her wary of everyone. But she knew, deep down, Vivian could be trusted. *And now I've fucked it up for good.* There was no coming back from this. A few careless words had destroyed any hope of a future with her.

She rose from the couch and stripped off the robe, laid it over the cushions, and went to her room. She crawled into bed and cried, huddled up on her side.

†

Vivian closed down her computer just as she heard the front door slam. She took a breath and stood, waiting for Lauren to appear. She'd left for work before Vivian had woken up. Vivian had been anxious all day for her to return. No doubt by now, Gregory would have called Lauren and told her what she'd done. She braced herself against the bedpost, knowing Lauren would be angry. A moment later, Lauren flung open the door, her face red, eyes blazing.

"Why would you do that?"

"Lauren, calm down."

"No, I won't calm down. What on earth were you thinking?"

I was thinking of you. Vivian let go of the post and settled on the mattress, memories of their lovemaking flashing through her mind. When she had walked out on Lauren in the lounge, her only thought had been to get as far away from her as possible. She'd lain awake for hours, planning on when to leave to go back to Cornwall. She'd had enough of being in the middle and wanted to take herself out of the equation. She knew if she left, Gregory would pull his funds. At that point, Vivian didn't care. She was hurt, angry, and humiliated. But as she cried, trying to fall asleep, she couldn't get Lauren out of her head. She didn't want to leave. She wanted Lauren next to her, making love with her. Vivian needed to find another plan. Inspiration struck at four o'clock. It was a risk, but one she had to take. Judging by Lauren's angry pacing in front of her, the plan had worked.

"I didn't have a choice. I wasn't going to be made to feel like I was using you, all for the sake of a job."

"So you told him you'd quit working for him if he didn't stop requesting reports on me? Vivian, that's crazy. He could just as easily fire you and take the funding away anyway."

"But at least you would know I wasn't using you."

Lauren stopped her pacing, her eyes wide as she stared at her. "You did this for me?" Vivian nodded. "Why? I was horrible to you."

"I know you didn't mean it. You were upset, and rightly so. I said from the beginning it would end in tears, and I was right. I don't want to work for him anymore anyway, but he doesn't know that. He still thinks we're great friends, and don't forget his crush on me. I thought that if I threatened to leave if he didn't stop spying on you, he would back down. And I was right. He wasn't happy about it, but he said he couldn't lose me. He says I'm the best CFO he's ever worked with."

Lauren blew out a breath. She perched on the office chair. "You took a big risk. How do you know he won't pull the funding?"

"He did say he would, but I convinced him not to."

"How?"

Vivian frowned. This was the part she wasn't proud of. She had done the thing Lauren had accused her of, except with Gregory and not Lauren. "I asked him not to. I said that he is such a generous man for helping you out and any woman would be lucky to be on his arm. I said I wish I could find someone like him."

"You flirted with him?"

"Yes. He suggested that when I get back, we go on a date."

Lauren's face paled, her hands trembling. "You're going to date my father?"

"What? God no." Vivian rushed over to Lauren, taking her hands in her own. "I agreed to a date, but I'm not going to go." The thought made her skin crawl. "Lauren, don't you see? This way you get to keep the project going. He's now off your back, and we can continue seeing each other. If that's what you want."

"But what about when you go home? I'll still be living here for the foreseeable future. He'll try to get to you. I'd rather pull the plug myself than put you in the position of having him court you. That would kill me."

Vivian reached up, cupping Lauren's cheek, brushing away the tear that fell. "I won't be going back there once this is over with. He won't get the chance."

"You don't know him as I do."

"It's a risk I'm willing to take. Lauren, I know how much all of this has upset you. Your mum dying, finding out about your real dad, and Gregory using me to spy on you. You've been strong through it all, but it isn't fair. You deserve to be happy. You deserve to live your life free of any pain." Vivian shook her head. "I don't want to add to that pain by giving you any reason to question my loyalties."

"You're the only one who makes it better."

"We can make this work. I told him everything up here is under control, and I'm looking forward to coming home. He has no reason to suspect anything. We can continue, together."

Lauren stood from the chair, crossing over to the window. It was dark outside. Light rain spattered against the windows. She didn't speak for a long moment. Vivian got to her feet and waited a little longer. She had risked everything for whatever Lauren was about to say. She didn't pretend she wasn't feeling sick with the waiting. Her stomach was in knots. Finally, Lauren spoke, her back still to Vivian.

"I don't know why you would do this for me." Lauren turned, smiling. "From the moment I met you, something inside clicked into place. It was like my heart recognised its soul mate. I know I've been angry and moody. I know I've hurt you, but I promise I'll try, every day, to make you happy. Thank you for doing this. You have no idea how much it means to me."

"I do." Vivian stepped forward. "Because I'm falling in love with you, and I will do anything I can to make you happy."

"Please forgive me."

Vivian gathered Lauren close as she wept, kissing the top of her head. "It's okay. We'll work it out. Just no more doubt between us."

"I promise. I'm so sorry."

"It's all right." Vivian led them to the bed, settling on top of the mattress. She didn't care that Lauren was still in her work clothes. Sheets could be washed. Holding Lauren and reconnecting with her was more important than clean bedding. Her gamble had paid off, but she was under no illusion their problems with Gregory were over. She just hoped they had time to build their relationship before it all came crashing down.

CHAPTER TEN

Over the next couple of weeks, Vivian and Lauren settled into a routine. Vivian would work for Bridger Holdings during the day, while Lauren went to the site. In the evening, they would spend their time talking and making love, occasionally going out for dinner. Gregory had kept his promise, not requesting an update about the project from Vivian. He still called and emailed about normal business, occasionally asking how Lauren was, but never about the project or what Lauren was personally doing. Vivian never got the sense he was after dirt on her. Vivian hated having to suck up to him, but it was the only way to guarantee his continued funding of the build.

Now into the second month, the new façade had begun. The spot for the pool had been dug, and all the underground plumbing systems were installed. Everything was on track, despite the odd day when work would stop due to torrential rain. Lauren predicted the outer building would be complete by the beginning of next month, and the inside could be started.

Vivian was sat at her computer, running through last month's numbers, checking there were no discrepancies before sending her report off to Gregory. Her phone buzzed next to her keyboard. She glanced at the caller ID. Terry, the architect, flashed up. Vivian frowned, having no idea why he would be calling her. Usually, if there was a problem at the site that needed Vivian's input, Lauren would call. Her heart beat a little faster as she reached for the phone, thinking there was something wrong with Lauren.

"Hello."

"Ms. Westfall? It's Terry. Is Lauren there? I have an idea about moving the showers closer to the pool that would look better in the final design."

"She isn't here. She left for work a couple of hours ago." Vivian didn't see her leave, but she did feel Lauren's lips on her forehead as she slipped out of bed that morning before the sun came up.

"That's odd. She hasn't been here all day. She texted me first thing, saying she couldn't make it today. I tried calling her mobile, but it's switched off."

Vivian stood from the chair forcefully, sending it sliding back against the bed. She was in full panic mode. *She could have had an accident. She could be dead.* "She didn't say anything to me last night before we went to bed. I assumed

113

she was there. I'll check the house and call you back." She didn't wait for his reply, ending the call and shoving the phone into her trousers. She rushed from the room and noticed Lauren's door was closed. She grabbed the handle and twisted, pushing the door wide. Relief flooded her, and her whole body turned to jelly as the fear of losing Lauren seeped from her bones. Lauren was curled up on her side, facing away from Vivian, head tucked to her chest. Vivian rushed around the other side of the bed and dropped to her knees. She reached out and grasped Lauren's shoulder.

"Lauren, honey. What's wrong?" Lauren opened her eyes, the whites red and bloodshot. The blanket beneath her head was damp from the tears she had shed. She didn't answer. She unfolded her arms from across her waist and held out a photograph. Vivian took the faded photo and studied the image. It was easy to recognise Lauren, even though she was a good twenty years younger. A woman stood next to her, arms around Lauren, their twin smiles shining for the camera. This was Lauren's mother. Vivian looked back at Lauren, the date resonating in her mind. "It's been a year, hasn't it?" Lauren nodded slightly, screwing her eyes shut as more tears fell. "Oh, baby." Vivian stood and retrieved her phone from her pocket. She dialled Terry's number. "Hi, Terry. Lauren's here. She's not feeling well. Can you leave this for another day?"

"Sure. It was just an idea. I can talk to her about it tomorrow. Hope she feels better soon."

"Thanks." Vivian hung up and tossed her phone onto the nightstand. She got onto the bed with Lauren, lifted her arm, and pulled Lauren close. Lauren sobbed as she huddled into Vivian. Vivian didn't talk, just held her while she cried.

She'd known the anniversary was coming up. She just hadn't realised it was today. Her tears slipped free in the wake of Lauren's grief.

"I'm sorry," Lauren whispered, her voice etched with heartbreak.

"You don't need to apologise. Just stay with me here and let me hold you."

Lauren sunk farther into Vivian's arms, Vivian's shirt soon becoming damp from Lauren's tears. A long while later, Lauren pulled back, wiping her face with her sleeve. She took a shuddering breath, not looking at Vivian. "I'm sorry," she said again. "I didn't think I'd get like that."

Vivian reached out and took Lauren's hand. "I said it's okay. Why didn't you come to me when you got upset?"

Lauren shrugged, glancing at her and then away. "I got up and came in here to get ready for work. I noticed the picture on my nightstand. I had completely forgotten what day it was. I took the photo and just crumpled onto the bed. I can't believe she's not here anymore."

"I know it's hard, but it will get easier." A flash of anger zipped over Lauren's features. Vivian squeezed her hand gently. "I know that sounds trite, but it's true. I miss my dad every day, but it's not as heartbreaking as it once was."

Lauren glared at her, top lip pulled between her teeth as if stopping herself from saying something she might later regret. After a few seconds, she sighed deeply and released her lip. "You're probably right, but right now, it feels like I've lost her all over again."

"Tell me what I can do to make this better for you."

"There's nothing." Lauren scooched to the edge of the bed. She stood, taking the photo of her mother with her. "I just want to be alone."

Vivian heard the bathroom door close quietly. Despite what Lauren said, there was no way Vivian would let her cope with this all on her own. They were lovers now, and that meant supporting each other, even when things were tough. She went to the kitchen and made a pot of coffee, waiting for Lauren to finish in the shower. Lauren appeared ten minutes later, her cheeks pink from the heat of the water, her hair swept back from her face. She wore Vivian's robe, bringing a quick smile from Vivian's lips.

"Feeling better?" Vivian asked.

Lauren nodded and sat at the island, her hands cradling the mug of coffee Vivian had set in front of her. "I guess I should get to the job site."

"No, not today. Terry can take care of things. Today is about you. Why don't we go somewhere, take a walk, and you can tell me about your mother."

Lauren screwed her face up as if that was the worst idea ever. "I said I want to be alone."

"And then you said you were going to work. Why won't you let me help you?" Vivian reached across the island, intent on holding Lauren's hand, but Lauren quickly hid them from view.

"I don't need your help." Lauren stood, knocking the stool over. She turned to leave but Vivian was quicker and blocked her path of escape.

Vivian grasped her biceps. "Why not?" Lauren struggled to break free, but Vivian was stronger. "Tell me."

"I don't like you seeing me like this."

"Like what?"

"Weak."

Vivian gasped, dropping her hands from Lauren's arms. Thankfully, Lauren didn't run. "You are not weak."

"I feel like it. I'm crying like a baby."

"Don't you think I did the same when my father died? I stayed in bed for three days. It's not weak to mourn the loss of a parent."

"I know, but I want to be strong in front of you. I feel like you keep having to rescue me. From my dad, from myself. I want to be your equal, not someone you feel responsible for."

"You know I don't feel that way."

Lauren's brows furrowed as she shook her head. "You must. You've done everything to help me, and I keep lapping it up. It's not fair."

"You think you're using me."

Lauren nodded.

"Like your father does?" Lauren flinched as if Vivian had slapped her. "Lauren, how could you think you're anything like him?" Vivian stepped forward, raising her hands to cup Lauren's cheeks and tilting her head to capture her gaze. "Everything I have done, I have done because I wanted to. You haven't manipulated me into doing anything I didn't want." Vivian moved her hand to Lauren's chest, above her heart. "I did it all because of who you are in here. I want to help you now, because you're upset. I want to help you through it, because I care about you. You'd do the same for me." A tear slipped from Lauren's eye. Vivian softened her voice. "You could never be like Gregory."

117

Lauren collapsed forward into Vivian, her arms wrapping tightly around her waist as she sobbed. "I hate how much I need you. I worry you'll see me for who I really am and leave."

"I know who you are, Lauren. I like who you are. Nothing you could do could push me away."

"I want to believe you, but I can't."

Vivian kissed her cheek. "Only time will prove I'm not going anywhere."

"Promise?"

"I promise." It was a silly thing to promise. Vivian had no idea what the future would bring, especially when Gregory found out about them. But in this moment, holding Lauren in her arms as she cried, she would pledge anything if it would ease some of her torment. "Now, how about we grab something quick to eat and go for that walk?"

Lauren pulled back, nodding. "I'd like that. I'll just go get changed." She leaned in and kissed Vivian quickly on the mouth. "I don't deserve you."

"Yes, you do." Vivian smiled reassuringly at her. "Just don't hide anything from me."

"I won't." Lauren took two steps away but stopped. "Thank you for being here for me."

"Always."

†

Vivian went through to the kitchen to put the kettle on as Lauren started the fire. They had walked up the high hill Lauren had pointed out from the lookout bluff. It had been a nice day, if not somewhat sombre. Lauren talked about her mother a lot, and Vivian felt it had brought her closer to knowing the woman she was falling for. Vivian pulled two mugs from the cabinet just as Lauren appeared.

"Hey, is the fire ready?"

Lauren nodded. "Yeah. Shouldn't take too long to warm through."

"We can put the radiators on if you like."

"Do you know what? I think I'd like to get into my PJs, grab the blankets from the bed, and lie in front of the fire."

"That sounds perfect. You go change, and I'll make the coffee." Vivian reached for the coffee jar. She felt Lauren's arm around her waist.

"Viv, I want to thank you for today." Lauren glanced away for a second. "I wasn't very nice to you this morning, but you helped me anyway."

"Lauren." Vivian put her fingers to Lauren's lips to stop her apology. It wasn't needed. "You are going through something painful. You didn't upset me or hurt me. I understand why you feel the way you do, but you have nothing to worry about. Okay?"

Lauren nodded but didn't pull away, her gaze turning sultry. "We won't need the heat on in the bedroom."

"No?" Vivian raised her eyebrows, knowing exactly what Lauren alluded to.

"No. I plan to heat you up perfectly."

Vivian's skin flushed, as Lauren drew lips across her jaw. "You already have. We might need to turn the fire off."

Lauren kissed her chin, then stepped away. "I'll get changed and sort the lounge out. I'll see you there."

Vivian watched her swagger away. Vivian took a breath, trying to cool herself down. She didn't think she would ever get enough of Lauren's teasing, or her body. *I never want to let her go.* She knew there were going to be problems in the future, but she didn't care. All she wanted was to lie down with Lauren on top of her, making her come for the rest of the night. With that plan in mind, she finished making the coffee and headed to her room to change. As she stepped inside, she noticed the email icon flashing on her monitor. In her haste to find Lauren that morning, she hadn't logged off from the system or told Gregory she would be out for the day. Her feet were heavy as she moved over to the computer. *Fourteen unread emails.* She glanced at her mobile sitting on the desk. That, too, had messages and missed calls. All were from Gregory asking if she was okay. *Shit.* She flopped into the chair cradling her phone. *What am I going to tell him?*

"Everything okay?" Lauren appeared in her doorway, wearing very little. Vivian couldn't stop her gaze from drifting down her torso and long legs. Lauren entered fully, concern in her eyes. "What's up?"

Vivian swallowed hard. Lauren's go-to emotion when talking about her father was always anger. Vivian knew this time wouldn't be any different. "When Terry called this morning to say you hadn't turned up for work, I rushed to find you. I didn't think about logging off the computer or informing Gregory I needed the day off. I forgot my phone when we went out." Vivian chanced a look at Lauren, trying to gauge her reaction. "He's been trying to get in touch all day."

"I wonder why he didn't call me. I had my phone." Lauren sat on the edge of the bed, close to Vivian. "Then again, he probably isn't concerned for me. What will you tell him?"

"You're not angry?"

"What? Why would I be?"

Vivian put her phone down and swivelled the chair so she could face her. She shrugged a shoulder. "Just going by past experience."

Lauren smirked. "Are you saying I'm difficult?"

Vivian matched her grin. "It has been known a time or two."

"I've had a good day, despite being an emotional wreck for most of it. I'm tired of letting him wind me up. He can't change his behaviour, but I can change how I react to it. I don't want to always be angry around you. I told you I want to make you happy. Flying off the handle over him won't help that. Now, what will you tell him? You can't blame the internet going down again, not when he couldn't reach you by phone."

"I guess I'll say I got food poisoning and have been in the bathroom all day. That should stop any further questions."

"Good idea." Lauren stood. "I'll be in the living room when you're done."

"You're not going to stay and listen?"

"Nope. I've got a nice warm fire to sit in front of."

Vivian laughed, and once Lauren was out of earshot, dialled Gregory's number. It went to his answerphone, so she left a message. She also sent an email, in case he didn't check his messages. With that sorted, she changed out of her jeans and jumper and into a skimpy pair of underwear. She left her chest bare, her nipples hardening in the cold of the room. It wouldn't be long before Lauren thoroughly warmed her up.

CHAPTER ELEVEN

"I don't know about you, but I'm getting hungry." Lauren threaded the soft strands of Vivian's hair through her fingers. They were cuddled together on the floor. The bungalow was silent, save for the crackle as the fire died down to embers. The day had started horribly for Lauren, realising it was her mother's anniversary. The crushing weight of her death had propelled her onto the mattress, where she'd lain crying for hours until Vivian found her. By day's end, Lauren felt much lighter. She smiled, knowing she was blessed to have Vivian by her side, helping her through the grief.

Their lovemaking had been hot and frantic; Lauren couldn't get enough. For the time being, they were satiated.

Lauren's stomach growled, reminding her the *other* appetite needed taking care of.

"I could eat." Vivian lifted her head from Lauren's chest, catching Lauren's gaze. "I'm not sure I can move, though. You keep wearing me out."

Lauren laughed. "I hope not too much. Once I have been fed, I plan on having you as dessert."

"Sounds perfect." Vivian took a deep breath and sat upright, her hair falling around her shoulders. "I'm going to drag myself to the shower. Why don't you throw some clothes on and go for pizza and wine? I fancy something warming."

"It's freezing out." Lauren was molten inside, her limbs heavy. She had no intention of going anywhere. She'd be happy with toast.

"It'll help cool you down."

Lauren mock glared at Vivian. "What do I get as a reward if I go?"

"Hmm, let's see." Vivian leaned in and captured Lauren's nipple in her mouth, biting gently, while her hand cupped Lauren's centre. "More of this?"

Lauren closed her eyes, concentrating on the feel of Vivian touching her. Her legs shook with the effort of tamping down her impending orgasm. It did no use. Vivian slipped her fingers inside and Lauren climaxed. She wasn't usually so quick to come, but with the hours of lovemaking, she was hypersensitive. Vivian's hand slipped away.

"You drive a hard bargain," Lauren said, her breathing ragged.

Vivian smiled and stood. "Go, before I change my mind." She disappeared around the corner. A moment later, the shower came on.

Lauren stayed where she was for a few minutes, reclining on the floor. She needed a moment to get the blood back into her legs. She got to her feet and went to her room. She slipped on her jogging bottoms and a comfy jumper, forgoing underwear. The minute she got back, she planned on being naked again. No sense in taking longer than necessary to undress. She had just reached for her car keys on the kitchen island, when there was a knock at the door. Lauren frowned, noting the time on the clock above the cooker. It was nearing nine. She had no idea who would be out there at this time of night. She opened the door, immediately cursing herself for not checking the peephole.

"Dad! What are you doing here?"

Gregory looked her up and down, then glanced behind her into the living room. Anyone with eyes could see this wasn't the normal set up for two people who were only roommates. The blankets were all jumbled up, the clothes Lauren had put on after her shower were tossed around the room. Add the lack of lighting and the dwindling fire, it was clear something had been going on. Gregory didn't comment. He pursed his lips and narrowed his eyes.

"Aren't you going to invite me in?" He stepped forward, pushing Lauren back with his forearm. He glanced around the room again, then back at Lauren. "I couldn't get in touch with Vivian, and I was worried. Where is she?"

"Hey, Lauren," Vivian called from the hall. "Don't forget, when you get back...Gregory!" Vivian appeared in the archway leading to the kitchen, her eyes wide. Lauren inwardly cursed, again. Vivian had on only a thin T-shirt that stopped mid-thigh, which Lauren recognised as one of her own. Her legs were bare, her hair wet from the shower. "What, um, what are you doing here?" She folded her arms across her chest, hiding her protruding nipples. Lauren didn't miss Gregory's predatory stare. She stepped around him and in front of Vivian, hoping to block his view of her.

"I was just telling Lauren I was worried when I couldn't get in touch with you. I thought it best to come check, make sure you were okay."

"I left you a message. I got, ah, food poisoning."

"Yes, I heard, but by then I was already halfway here. No sense in turning around. Besides, that'll give me a chance to have a look at the project."

Lauren's hands balled into fists. She wanted to throw him out, tell him to stick his money and never bother them again. *How dare he show up here like this.* The touch of Vivian's fingers on her back helped calm her. It would do no good to get pissy with him. *He's here now. I'll have to put up with it.*

"It's too late to go now," Lauren said, trying to make her voice come off as pleasant.

Gregory waved his hand. "Oh, I know that. I've booked a room in town. I'll meet you there tomorrow, say around eleven? Afterward, I'd like to take Vivian to lunch, if you're feeling better. I have a few things I need to discuss with you."

"That sounds fine," Vivian said, her hand still on Lauren. "I'm feeling a lot better now anyway."

"Yes, you do look quite relaxed." Gregory raised an eyebrow, tilting his head slightly to indicate the mess in the lounge.

"Oh, um, yeah. I couldn't get warm, so Lauren suggested I lie by the fire. She's been taking really good care of me."

"I don't doubt it." His gaze cut to Lauren, a flash of anger shining from his eyes. "I must be going. I need to check in. Tomorrow at eleven, Lauren?"

Lauren nodded.

"Good. Vivian, don't worry about logging into the network tomorrow. Take the morning off. I'll be here around twelve to pick you up."

"Okay."

"Well, goodnight."

Lauren didn't see him out. She refused to move, belligerent to the fact he had shown up unannounced. Had he been there fifteen minutes earlier, he would have interrupted Vivian giving her an orgasm. The door shut quietly, and Lauren sighed heavily.

"You don't think he knows about us, do you?" Vivian walked to the window and pulled the curtain aside, peering into the darkness.

Lauren sat on the sofa, head in her hands. "It doesn't take a genius to work it out."

"You don't have to be so sarcastic. I'm worried."

Lauren looked up. "Vivian, look at this place. Your underwear is on the bloody coffee table. He isn't stupid."

"What are we going to do?"

Lauren shook her head, lost for words. She held on to the glimmer of hope that he hadn't figured it out, but that was a fool's dream. Gregory Bridger was a very smart man. There was no doubt in her mind he knew exactly what they had been doing.

"He didn't blow a gasket," Lauren said. "So maybe he doesn't care."

"You don't believe that, do you?"

"No. My best guess is he'll go to his hotel and come up with a plan to get you away from here. He'll probably stop the project."

Vivian rushed over and dropped to her knees in front of Lauren, her eyes glistening with unshed tears. "We can't let him do that."

"We won't have a choice."

"What if we just tell him that we're dating? That we like each other."

Lauren smiled sadly, raising her hand to brush away the tear that rolled down Vivian's cheek. "You don't really believe it'll be that simple, do you?"

"We're both grown adults. He can't control us."

"How many times do I have to tell you that you don't know Gregory Bridger? He'll stop at nothing to get what he wants. And what he wants is *you*."

"He doesn't own me."

"Not yet, but he will."

Vivian shot to her feet, angrily wiping at her face. "I can't believe you're willing to give up this easily."

Lauren slouched back into the cushions. "We knew it would come to this. It's my fault for pushing you into the relationship."

"You didn't push me into anything. I was just as much attracted to you as you were me. I refuse to be bullied by him."

"There's nothing we can do about it now."

Vivian stared at her for a moment. "I'm tired. I'm going to bed."

Lauren heard the bedroom door slam, shutting away the one person who had ever stirred anything in her heart. It was over. She knew her father. Whatever plan he came up with, would surely take Vivian away for good. He wouldn't ever have Vivian, and he probably knew that, but he would do what he could to make sure Lauren didn't have her either.

She stood from the couch, then folded up the blankets. She made sure the fire was out and locked the doors. She went down the hall, stopping outside Vivian's door. She wanted to go in, to lie down with her and have one more night of holding her. However, she turned away and entered her own room. Spending the night together would only lead to more heartache.

As she lay in her own bed, she thought she would be devastated that the project would go unfinished, that her dream would never be fulfilled. But all she cared about was that the woman she had fallen in love with was now gone from her life. Nothing could stop Gregory Bridger when he set his mind on something.

†

"You've done a most excellent job, Lauren," Gregory said, as Lauren led him off the site. She had spent the last hour showing him around. He seemed genuinely interested in the progress she had made, asking lots of questions and making suggestions. If Lauren didn't know any better, she would have thought he cared. *Maybe he does and I'm just being hard on him.* So far, he hadn't mentioned the previous night, and that was fine with Lauren. "I had no idea how far you'd gotten in just a few weeks," he continued. "Terry thinks we can start arranging delivery of the interior materials. He sees no problem why we shouldn't be ready to go in a couple of weeks." She was impressed that no problems had arisen. They had only needed to close the site twice due to bad weather. Other than that, it was running smoothly. She had no doubt they would meet the proposed opening date of the first of June.

Gregory clasped her shoulder, his gaze penetrating. He smiled at her. "I'm proud of you, Lauren. I know I don't say it often, but it's true."

"Thanks, Dad." Lauren looked away. He had never said that to her before, and it made her wary.

"Right, before I go, I need to talk to you about something important. Come sit with me in the car."

Lauren followed him to his Mercedes, her stomach clenching, threatening to throw up the toast she'd had for breakfast. The reprieve from talking about last night was over. She settled into the passenger side, keeping her face forward. She didn't want to look at him. "What's up?"

"It's Vivian."

Lauren briefly closed her eyes. He didn't sound angry. His voice was calm and quiet. That worried her more than if he'd bellowed at her. "What about her?"

"I don't know what you're playing at, but it has to stop."

"Why?"

Gregory sighed, his hand lightly grasping the steering wheel. "Lauren, Vivian is very important to the company. I value her expertise. I'm concerned that once this thing with you is over, she'll want to leave. I can't have you running off my best employee, all because you couldn't keep your hands to yourself."

He sounded reasonable enough, but Lauren knew that wasn't the real reason. She recalled the way her father had spoken to her at his Christmas party. Even Damien could see he was threatening toward her. This wasn't about business; this was about him having Vivian to himself.

"Why do you assume it'll end?"

"Come on. We both know you don't have it in you for a long-term relationship. And don't forget your plan to open a chain of these spas." He motioned his hand toward the site. "You can't work all those hours and maintain a relationship. Trust me, it doesn't work. One or the other will suffer. Do you really want to do that to her?"

Despite knowing what he said was a way to get her to back away from Vivian for his own gain, she couldn't help but concede his point. Lauren would be in Scotland for at least the rest of the year, making sure everything ran smoothly, while working on her plan for the next branch to open. He was right, she wouldn't have time to see Vivian. Especially with Vivian being at the other end of the country. It didn't matter how much Lauren wanted to be with her, it wouldn't work. "Of course not, but—"

"No. No buts. It's time for you to grow up and be the woman you were raised to be."

"You know nothing about me." She didn't know why she was arguing with him, but she didn't want to give him the satisfaction of winning without a fight. If things ended with Vivian, it would be because they decided to end it, not Gregory.

"Lauren, this isn't a request. I'm telling you it's over between you. If you don't finish it, I will."

"I'm not a child, Dad. You can't force me to do something I don't want to do." Lauren looked at him for the first time since getting in the car. His face was relaxed, almost kind. For a moment, Lauren thought maybe he did care. But then his eyes narrowed, and he pulled his lips into a tight line. His hand on the steering wheel gripped tighter.

"Then say goodbye to your little project."

"Go ahead, take it away. I'll find something else to do. I won't be blackmailed into ending it with her. I love her."

"Don't make me laugh." His whole body shook as he guffawed. He wiped the tears from his eyes and then glared at her. "You do, don't you?"

Lauren nodded. "Yes."

"Then you are a fool. There is no way she feels the same way about you."

"You know nothing about us. I won't sit here and let you try and bully us into doing what you want."

Gregory glanced at the clock on the dashboard. "Look at the time. I must be going." He smirked. "I have a lunch date to keep."

He nodded his head at her door. Lauren grasped the handle. There would be no winning with him, not today. "Don't you dare say anything to her."

"What I discuss with my CFO is of no concern of yours. Get back to your little project, while you still can."

Lauren stepped from the car, then watched as he tore away from the site, the tyres spraying mud in the air behind him. The cold wind penetrated Lauren's work jacket and straight through to her heart. She knew he would convince

131

Vivian to walk away from her. She debated jumping in her car and chasing after him to stop him from getting to Vivian. It would be useless. He would find a way to get to her eventually. Lauren just needed to hope that Vivian was strong enough to not listen to whatever lies he told her. He didn't even seem to care Vivian was gay. All he wanted was to have her to himself and away from Lauren. This was no longer about his own feelings for Vivian, but an attempt to sabotage Lauren's happiness.

†

Vivian glanced at the clock and sighed. Noon. Gregory would arrive any minute to take her to lunch. She had never felt such dread before. Not only was she highly embarrassed he knew she was sleeping with Lauren, but she feared this meeting would signal the end to their relationship. *Well, Lauren said it was over anyway. Why should I worry what Gregory says?* She had cried well into the early hours. The past few weeks had been the most precious of her life. Spending every night with Lauren had been everything Vivian had ever wanted. Sure, she knew they had difficulties coming in the future, a long-distance relationship being one of them, but she had thought they would work them all out. Even Gregory finding out didn't worry her as much as it did in the beginning. However, it was clear Lauren didn't feel the same sense of hope. When she told Vivian it was over between them, Vivian thought her heart would smash right out of her chest. She had never expected the devastating blow. She couldn't help but wonder if this was all just a fling for Lauren, something to pass the time while they were holed up in wintry Scotland. *No. The way she holds me, touches me. You can't fake that kind of connection.* Vivian refused to believe that was all there was between them. *She might be willing to give up on us, but I'm not.* The knocking on the door startled her even though she was waiting for it. She stood from the couch and opened the door. Gregory stood before her, his smile wide and bright.

"Ah, Vivian. You look delightful. Shall we?"

He stepped back and held out his arm for her to take. She grabbed her bag from the armchair and reluctantly hooked her hand into the bend of his arm, allowing him to lead her to his car.

"Where are we going?" she asked after he had been driving for ten minutes.

"My hotel. I glanced over their menu last night. Their steak options look lovely, so I thought we'd eat in the restaurant."

"Okay." Vivian turned her head to look out the window, watching the trees and occasional house go by. Gregory seemed content to drive in silence, but Vivian's nerves wouldn't allow it. She was desperate to find out how the meeting went with Lauren and what was said if anything. "How did it go at the job site?"

"It's looking really good. Lauren has done amazingly."

Vivian pulled her brows down, frowning as she did so. He sounded pleased, which was at odds to how he had expressed his doubt in Lauren's ability from the start. "Yes, she has. She knows what she's doing."

"Just as you predicted. It would be a shame for it all to disappear."

"What do you mean?" Vivian's heart beat faster, knowing exactly what he was alluding to, but wanting him to acknowledge it out loud.

"Oh, nothing. Here we are." He pulled up into a space outside the hotel. Vivian stared up at the massive building through the windshield. It had to be the largest hotel in all of Scotland. *Trust Gregory to stay in the most expensive place going.* She stepped from the car, taking Gregory's arm again, and entered the lobby. He led her off to the left and into the restaurant.

"Table for two, please," Gregory said to the maître d.

They were shown to a secluded table by a large window overlooking the grounds of the hotel. Two large sculptures spewed streams of water into an intricate pattern over a large stone pool, surrounded by neatly trimmed grass and shrubs. It would be a pleasant view, if not for the company she was in.

"Please sit." Gregory pulled out her chair for her. Vivian took off her coat and laid it over the back of the chair. A young, blond waiter approached, order pad in hand. "Wine?"

Vivian nodded. It was a little early for alcohol, but she needed something to get through this. "Thank you."

"Two Selkirk's sauvignon blanc," Gregory told their waiter. "Thank you." The waiter nodded, then left. "Now, before we order, I need to talk to you about Bridger Holdings. A rumour has come to my attention, and I need your help on the matter."

"What's the problem?" Vivian clamped her hands tightly together under the table. She still didn't know if Gregory had spoken to Lauren about them, and the wait was killing her.

Gregory was acting like he didn't know about them. *If only that were true.*

"Edward, from the collections department, has been skimming off the top."

"What? That's impossible." There was no chance anyone could be stealing from the company. Vivian kept such a religious eye on all the accounts. She checked every receipt, every payment and statement. She doubled checked her work, and every column added up perfectly. No one could be taking money from the company.

"I thought so, too. From what I can gather, he's adding half a percent of interest to the loans on top of the agreed amount. The client has paid what he requested, but he only enters the correct amount into the accounts. I don't know how he's doing it. I checked the system, but can't find anything amiss. That's where you come in. I need you to come back to Cornwall and audit his department, see if you can find out if this rumour is true."

"But what about my work here?"

"We both know I sent you here to keep an eye on Lauren. You haven't reported back to me in weeks, and she's doing a good job. I can trust her here on her own. You're no longer needed in Scotland."

The waiter approached and set two glasses down in front of them. He poured an inch of wine into Gregory's glass. He took a sip and nodded. The waiter poured their drinks and walked away. Vivian took a large gulp. She put her glass down and refocused on Gregory.

"What about the accounts? I'm supposed to be in charge of them." It was a lame excuse. Lauren hadn't needed supervision since they arrived. She was more than capable of running things there without her. The truth was Vivian didn't want to leave. She wanted to continue spending her nights with Lauren, making love and talking.

"I said I can trust her. I'll put her name on the account, and she can run it as she sees fits. I was wrong to doubt her. I'm so very proud of the work she's doing." Gregory squinted his eyes slightly. "Lauren agrees she'll be okay on her own."

"She said that?"

"Yes. We did have a few cross words. She hated that I sent you to spy on her, but she accepted my apology. All she wants now is to get stuck into the project without distractions."

"Distractions?" Vivian blinked, unsure she'd heard right. *She said I was a distraction.* She stared at Gregory, trying to see if she could spot his lie. He stared back, unflinching. Vivian had worked with him enough to recognise his mannerisms. He was being sincere.

"Yes. Lauren has never been very good at multitasking. She has a very short attention span. With you gone, she'll be able to carry on and get the spa open on time."

"So, you know about us?" Her cheeks flamed from embarrassment.

"Vivian, I may be a lot older than you, but I know some things about the world. I don't blame you for falling for her charms. She can be very persuasive when she wants to be. But it's time for the fun to stop and the work to begin. She agrees."

Vivian shook her head, desperately trying to cling onto the time they'd shared. Her feeling from earlier resurfaced, that all Lauren wanted was a fling to pass the time. "She wouldn't."

"I don't have time for games." Gregory leaned forward, resting his arms along the edge of the table. His gaze bored into Vivian's. "Let me put it in words you'll understand. If you don't come back to Cornwall tonight, I'll have no option but to pull my funding and end the project. Is that what you want?"

Vivian sucked in a breath. "You're blackmailing me?"

"You make it sound so nefarious." Gregory adjusted his position, straightening up in the chair. "I'm simply saying I need you back in the office, and Lauren needs to concentrate on her work up here. If neither one of you can do that, then I have no option but to secure my finances."

"I'm not hungry. Take me back to the cottage." She stood from the chair and put her coat on. She wouldn't sit there while Gregory tried to blackmail her into doing his bidding. The whole situation from the start had been a red flag. She was stupid to agree to any of it. But it had been worth the pain to spend the last month and a half with Lauren. Now, though, it was becoming too much of a game. She couldn't trust Gregory, and now she doubted she could trust Lauren.

Gregory stood and tossed a twenty-pound note onto the table. Vivian stalked from the building, Gregory keeping stride beside her. They settled into his car, and he drove them back in silence. He pulled up outside the cottage but left the engine running. Before Vivian had a chance to escape, he spoke.

"I'm sorry if this seems underhanded to you. But I won't have my business messed with."

For the first time since he arrived, his tone turned threatening. *This must be the Gregory Lauren warned me about.* She had never seen him look so fierce, not even in board meetings when the staff was underperforming. "Is there even a problem with Edward?" she asked.

"No. But it will sound good when you tell Lauren that's why you're leaving."

"I could quit."

"True. In which case, I still pull the funding. Do you want Lauren to lose the dream she's worked so hard for?"

Vivian wanted to believe that Lauren would give it all up for her but knew she never would. Building her chain of health clubs was her only way of validating her life. She wanted something to be proud of, to leave as a legacy. No way she would give all that up after six weeks of sleeping together. Vivian didn't want to be the cause of her losing it all. "Why are you doing this?"

"Did you think I didn't know what was going on up here? The missed emails, phone calls going unanswered. I knew, for certain, when you tried to blackmail me into not spying on her any longer."

Vivian had known at the time that blackmailing Gregory was a big risk. She had stupidly thought she had succeeded in getting him off their backs. "Why can't you just let us be happy?"

"She isn't right for you, Vivian. I'm protecting you from her."

"I don't need your protection."

"Well, you're getting it anyway. Come back tonight, and I'll allow her to continue her little project. If you don't, she'll lose it all. Drive safely. I'll see you first thing in the morning."

Vivian got out of the car and rushed inside, hearing Gregory pull away. She tore her coat off and ran to the bathroom. She made it just in time, before she threw up what little she had in her stomach. She leaned back against the tiled wall and drew her knees tight against her chest. The tears came, tumbling down her face and neck. She didn't bother wiping them away. Gregory hadn't left her any choice. She needed to walk away before he destroyed all of Lauren's hopes. Vivian wouldn't be the one to take it all away from her. Lauren had been through so much in her life. She couldn't rely on anyone, especially now her mother was gone. Lauren wouldn't admit it, but she was fragile. Building the spa gave her the confidence she was after. Who was Vivian to rip that all away? No, it was best all-around if she left and let Lauren get on with her life. Vivian would go back to Bridger Holdings, stick it out for as long as it took Lauren to pay Gregory back, then she would quit. It was the least she could do for her.

†

Vivian had just loaded the computer monitor into the boot of the car when she heard tyres crunching on gravel behind her. She shut the lid and turned in time to see Lauren's car roll to a stop. Lauren climbed and rushed over to Vivian.

"What are you doing?" Lauren's gaze went to the back seat, spotting the suitcases. "What did he say to you?"

139

"It doesn't matter." Vivian turned away and walked back inside. Lauren followed right behind her.

"What do you mean it doesn't matter? You're leaving, aren't you?"

Vivian sighed and folded her arms across her chest to stop herself from reaching out to Lauren. She couldn't. Any touch would be too much and break her resolve. She needed to be the strong one. "Yes. There is a problem at head office. Gregory needs me to come back so I can look into it."

"Bullshit." Lauren's nostrils flared, her eyes tightening. "You're lying."

"Lauren, don't make this any harder than it has to be. It's the best all-around if I go."

"Best for whom? Because it certainly isn't best for me."

"You need to concentrate on getting the health club finished. You can't do that if I'm around distracting you." Vivian headed into the bedroom, wanting to make sure she hadn't left anything behind. Again, Lauren followed.

"Distracting me? What are you on about?"

"Gregory is pleased with the progress you're making. You don't want to let him down."

"Screw him." Lauren reached out and grabbed Vivian's arm, turning her so they were face to face. "I don't give a damn about what he thinks. Why are you leaving?"

Vivian shook Lauren's hand off, taking a step back. "Look, we both knew it would come to this. It's just happening sooner rather than later. You need to get on with the project, and I need to get on with my life."

"I don't believe this. You were the one yesterday telling me we can make it work, and now you're running out on me."

"Stop being so dramatic. We had fun. Nothing more, nothing less." She stepped around Lauren and went back to the lounge. She lifted her coat off the armchair and threaded her arms through the sleeves, avoiding Lauren's gaze as she did so.

"You know that's not true. I love you."

Vivian's stomach clenched. She closed her eyes and swallowed hard. The words coated her soul, filling her with the need to take Lauren in her arms and kiss her. She wanted to say she loved her too, that they could figure this out, but she couldn't. She knew Gregory would make good on his threat. Vivian didn't want Lauren to lose everything. She opened her eyes, looking directly into Lauren's desperate gaze. "Well, I don't feel the same."

"Stop lying to me. Tell me what he said."

"Nothing I didn't already know."

"Which is?"

Vivian sighed. Lauren wasn't going to let it drop until she knew the truth. "If I stay, he'll cut the funding. Your dream will be over."

"I told you, I don't care about the health club. I care about you." Lauren took a step forward, her gaze softening.

"You say that now, but once I'm gone, in a few weeks, you won't even remember me."

"That's not true."

"I won't be the reason you lose the dream you've worked so hard for. I need to leave." Vivian turned her back and opened the front door. She stepped through, fishing her car keys from her pocket.

"You're letting him blackmail you," Lauren called after her.

141

"It might look that way, and yes he tried, but this isn't coming from him. This is my decision." She stopped at her car, glancing over her shoulder. "We had a great few weeks. It's over now."

"I can't believe you're doing this after everything you said."

"You said it yourself last night. Gregory will stop at nothing to get what he wants. It's easier to just go along with it. And he's right, we're not a good match." She opened the car door and got inside. Lauren's hand on the frame stopped her from pulling it closed. She crouched down so she could see Vivian at eye level.

"You don't really think that."

Vivian nodded. "I do. I need to get back to my proper job, and you need to stay here."

"If you walk away now, there's no going back."

"I know."

Lauren stood, a tear falling down her cheek. "Then go. Go work for that asshole. You deserve each other."

Vivian flinched, as Lauren slammed her car door. She put the key in the ignition and backed out of the driveway onto the main road, careful of any oncoming traffic. She glanced back up the driveway, expecting to see Lauren watching her leave. The drive was empty, save for Lauren's car. Vivian put the car in gear and pulled away. She gripped the steering wheel tightly, her breath coming in gasps. She pulled over into a bus stop and wept. Deep in her heart, she knew she was making a mistake, but she had to do everything she could to help Lauren succeed. It didn't matter her own heart was breaking. It would take time, but eventually, Lauren would get over her. She would be so busy with the health club she wouldn't even give Vivian a second thought. Vivian clung to that hope, because the thought of Lauren suffering the loss of her for more than a few days was more than Vivian could stomach. She had no doubt Lauren loved her. She loved Lauren too, but it was time to move on. They were doomed before they even began. Vivian should have stuck to her resolve to not get involved with her. Lauren had been too hard to resist, though, and now they were both suffering.

CHAPTER TWELVE

Lauren crossed the kitchen and chucked her empty beer bottle into the rubbish. She opened the fridge and grabbed another, twisting the cap off and throwing it to the side. She leaned back against the island, taking a long pull as she gazed out the window and into the late afternoon sun shrouded with clouds. The first of April had brought warmer, longer days. Now the good weather had arrived, the health club build was picking up speed. Everything was completed except the final install of gym equipment and soft furnishings. Lauren had spent her days on-site. In the evenings, she worked on planning the soft opening for a few select, potential clients. The local community and press would be invited to the grand opening the first of June. The soft opening was to gather some interest and make sure the facilities all worked properly. That was probably the only good thing about Vivian leaving. Lauren had been able to work day and night, resulting in no delays. *Perhaps Vivian was right. Perhaps she was a distraction.* Lauren shook her head. It had been six weeks since Vivian left, and Lauren hadn't heard a word from her. She had thought the two of them were in love, and that maybe it was hard for Vivian to walk away. As it turned out, Vivian didn't give a shit about her. Lauren assumed she still worked for Gregory, but her father never mentioned her. Lauren certainly wasn't going to bring her up. She had spoken to Gregory twice in the last few weeks and sent the occasional email containing pictures of the spa. They didn't speak about personal things, the same as usual.

She took her beer and went to the lounge. Someone knocked on the front door before she had the chance to sit down. A flutter of anticipation rose in her chest. She put her bottle down and rushed over to pull the door wide. She chided herself for her haste when she saw her guest was not Vivian.

"Damien, what are you doing here?" Her brother stood before her, dressed casually in chinos and a polo shirt. He smiled widely, showing perfect teeth. Lauren could tell they'd been whitened recently. He looked like the yacht owner he was, suited to the seas of the Caribbean and not the mostly grey skies of Scotland.

"Can't a brother visit his sister?"

"Of course." Lauren hugged him briefly, then stepped aside. "Come on in. How're the kids?"

"All good. Growing too fast. I came to see how the build is going." He glanced around the living room, then settled on the armchair. Lauren sat on the couch. "Dad showed me the progress pictures you sent him. It looks really good."

"It's all pretty much finished. We have the gym equipment arriving Tuesday and the furnishers Friday. It should all be ready for the soft opening in two weeks."

Damien leaned forward, resting his elbows on his spread knees. "You must be excited to see the end in sight."

"Yeah, it's been a busy few months." She tried to put as much energy into her reply as possible. It was hard. All she could see in her mind were images of Vivian.

"Must be why you look so worn out."

Lauren quirked an eyebrow. "How do you mean?"

"Not being funny, but it's clear you've lost weight. The smudges under your eyes are greyer than the clouds outside." He motioned his head toward the window behind him. She waved him off.

"You know how it is. Work, work, work."

Damien quirked his eyebrow the same as she had done, a trait they'd inherited from their mother. "Are you sure that's all there is to it?"

"Of course."

"You're not sick, are you?" He frowned, his brows now both pulling down.

"No, I'm fine. Hey, it's still light out. How about I give you the tour of the health club?"

"Sure, sounds great."

Lauren grabbed her keys and led Damien from the cottage. They chatted about nonsensical things as she drove, and before long, she pulled up outside the health club. The security screen that had encircled the property during the renovation was now gone. The building stood proud and elegant. The landscapers had been out the week before, adding the grass, shrubs, and gravel parking lot. The golf club could be seen in the distance, nothing but rolling hills and nice views between them. Lauren reflexively smiled. She never got tired of seeing her dream come to fruition. The melancholy arrived right after, knowing her dream came at a cost. She was proud of what she had achieved, but her heart wasn't in it anymore. Doubt swamped her, and she acknowledged her desire to flee.

She spent the next hour showing Damien around the inside, pointing out all the little details she'd added to make the place high class. She had thought of everything, from top-quality towels to intricate door handles. No expense had been spared to make this place bespoke and worthy of the membership fee. She ended the tour out in the grounds, sitting on a bench overlooking the water feature in the small gardens.

"I must say, Sis, you've done an amazing job. No wonder Dad is singing your praises."

"It's just a shame it's taken me doing this for him to stop being a jerk to me. And we both know it's all about appearances. He's probably telling his investors and clients how well *his* project is going." Damien cleared his throat, clueing her in that she was right. "He doesn't change, does he?"

Damien lightly touched her knee. "He's still proud of you. Don't forget he thought you'd fail."

"Yeah. Guess I proved him wrong." That brought her a modicum of satisfaction, but it didn't belay the fact he had taken away the most important person in her life. *When are you going to stop thinking about her all the time?* It was getting tiresome. Even when working, Vivian was always in her thoughts. Nighttime was even worse, when there was nothing to distract her. She often she stayed up working until the early hours just to wear her brain out enough to fall into an exhausted sleep. It wouldn't help, though. Vivian came to her in her dreams.

"Have you talked to him much?"

"Not really. I send him updates occasionally. Sometimes he'll email with a query about one of the invoices. Other than that, not a peep."

"Why would he query the invoices? I thought that was Vivian's job."

"She's still there, then?" Her hands gripped the edge of the bench.

"Yes, why wouldn't she be? She's working hard on the end of year accounts. Maybe that's why he's doing the queries on this."

"Maybe."

"Speaking of end of year accounts. April fifteenth is coming up in a couple of weeks. Dad's spring party. He wants you there."

"Then why didn't he send me an invitation?"

Damien looked away.

"Ah, that's why you're here."

"He was going to send one, but I offered to come up and see you. I wanted to check out the place anyway. So, will you be there?"

"I've still got a lot of work to do up here."

"It's just for a couple of days."

148

"I'm not sure I'm up to it." *Not if Vivian is going to be there.* Which she would be. The events of a year ago came forth. The kiss, Vivian's hand down her trousers, the smell of her perfume. That night had been the start of Lauren's new life. Two weeks short of a year later, she was heading back to square one. She didn't want to be up here anymore, but she didn't know where to go. France was an option, but that would be like going too far back into the past. She needed to move forward. She just didn't know where.

"Come on, Lauren. It's just one night."

"You know I suck at playing happy families."

"He'll be pissed if you don't show up."

"Isn't he always?" Damien shrugged, and Lauren sighed. "Fine, I'll be there." *If only for a glimpse of Vivian. One last look before I go on my way.*

"Great. Let's go grab a beer somewhere. I can tell you about my plans to expand into the jet ski business."

"I thought business was slow?"

"It was over winter, but I had some new orders come in recently. With summer coming up in a couple of months, I thought now would be the perfect time to branch out. Not everyone can afford a luxury yacht, but jet skis are affordable. Cheaper to make, and I'll sell more."

"Sounds like a good idea."

"It is. Come on."

As they strolled back to the car, an idea formulated in her mind. *If Damien's up for it, this could pave the way for me to get out from under our father and not be tied to anything here anymore.*

†

149

Vivian passed over a sheet of paper to Gregory, then pointed to the figure at the end of the column of numbers. "That's your bottom line. We're up six percent on last quarter and thirteen percent on the year."

"Wonderful." Gregory beamed, his smile almost verging on creepy. He looked up at Vivian with a calculating gaze. "This has been the best year yet. I think we should go ahead with opening an office in Australia. Lots of land there we could cultivate."

"Are you sure?" Vivian stepped around to the other side of the desk and sat in the guest chair. She crossed one leg over the other as she thought over his suggestion. "That's a big risk and will severely cut your profits for England and Europe next year."

"I think it's worth the risk, don't you?" He raised his eyebrows, tilting his head slightly as he did so.

"I can do some cost projection analyses, model our potential investment and profit or loss."

"You are a wizard with the numbers. I'm sure you can make it feasible."

"I'll try." She stood from the chair and straightened her jacket. It was coming up to eight in the evening, and all she wanted was to go home and open the bottle of white zin she had chilling in the fridge. She took two steps away before Gregory stopped her.

"Vivian?"

She glanced over her shoulder at him. "Yes?"

"Everything okay? You've not been the same since you got back."

Of course she wasn't okay. She had been forced to choose between her happiness and Lauren's success. She missed her terribly. Every night at home she opened her wine, drank until she couldn't keep her eyes open, and usually slept on the couch. She had to make sure to leave her mobile in the car overnight, so she wouldn't be tempted to call Lauren, even just to hear her voice. Lauren's distraught face the day Vivian left played itself over and over in a loop, along with Lauren's plea of "I love you." No, she wasn't okay. Vivian was damn well miserable. Coming into the office every day didn't help matters. Every time she had to meet with Gregory, she had to control her contempt for him. It didn't help he kept leering at her. She had never noticed it before Scotland, but now it was easy to see the gleam in his eyes and the way his gaze would sweep up her body. She wasn't sure how much longer she could stomach being at Bridger Holdings. There was only so much she could take.

"I'm not sure what you mean. I've done my job to the best of my ability. Everything is shaping up, ready for the year ahead."

"I didn't mean work wise. You seem sad, sullen almost."

Vivian marched back to the desk, leaning her hands on the edge and towering over Gregory who still sat in his chair. "Let's be frank. You forced me to walk away from Lauren. How did you expect me to be?"

"You know it was for the best. And you've seen the pictures. She's done an amazing job on the health club."

"Yes, as I knew she would." She straightened. "You didn't need to blackmail me."

"You still think that's what I was doing?" He narrowed his eyes, clasping his fingers together under his chin. "No, my dear. I simply made you see the bigger picture. Besides, we both know we work well together. Maybe we can—"

"Stop right there." Vivian held her hand out to forestall his next words. "If you say anything inappropriate, I'll have you up on sexual harassment charges."

Gregory's eyes widened, his brows raising practically into his hairline. He looked almost shocked she would ever suggest his interest was anything more than platonic. It was all a ruse, she knew. He was just shocked she called him on it. *He doesn't even seem to care that I'm a lesbian.*

"Vivian, I would never. You're my best friend's daughter. And twenty-five years younger, I might add. How could you think such a thing? I made a silent promise to your father's memory to look out for you. I would never do anything to hurt or upset you."

Bullshit! "You already have."

"Not this again." He sighed heavily and stood from his chair. "Vivian, Lauren wasn't right for you. You belong here, by my side. Together, we can become the biggest company in the world."

"I don't want that. I just want to do my job." *And get out of here as soon as I can.*

"Think about what I am offering you. I'm not suggesting anything romantic, but by my side, you can become a very wealthy woman. Nothing needs to change between us. However, the perception other people have of us will change."

Is he seriously suggesting we pretend we're partners? Vivian couldn't think of anything worse. There was no way on earth she would do that. Besides, what would it do to Lauren? "I'm not interested."

"Then I might have to think about your position here."

"You do that. I have had enough of you manipulating, blackmailing, and generally being an ass to last a lifetime."

"Careful, Vivian. I still have the power to end Lauren's little dream."

Vivian closed her eyes, defeated. She couldn't keep going along with all this. Lauren had been right. He would stop at nothing to get what he wanted. That didn't mean she would give it to him. If she quit, he would no longer be able to blackmail her. Lauren's face flashed through her mind. She thought of the first day Lauren showed her around the village. She had been so earnest, so excited to tell Vivian all about her designs and what she hoped to bring to the community. *Could I walk away and allow him to take that from her?* No, she couldn't. She had stuck it out this long. She might as well carry on and hope Lauren soon found a way of paying him back.

"I'll see you at the party tomorrow night." She strode from the room, ignoring Gregory's satisfied smirk. She closed her office door and leaned back against it, her breathing ragged. One bottle of wine wouldn't be enough. She'd be making a stop at the shop on the way home.

CHAPTER THIRTEEN

"Tonight is extra special," Gregory said from his position on the podium. He held a champagne glass loosely, as he spoke through the microphone. "Not only are we celebrating another profitable year, but my daughter Lauren is here to raise a glass to our new business venture." He looked over to the far side of the room. Vivian followed his gaze over the crowd of people. Her breath caught. Leaning up against the wall, Lauren looked magnificent in her white tux. After such a long time, Vivian hadn't expected the jolt seeing Lauren would bring. She swung her gaze back to Gregory as he continued. "The first health spa Lauren has project managed will be opening in just a few short weeks. She has done an amazing job of getting everything ready. So, I would like you all to join me in toasting Lauren and Bridger Holdings. May our success be long and prosperous."

The crowd toasted and cheered. Gregory bowed and left the stage. Vivian looked back over to Lauren, but she was gone. She felt a hand on her back, the gesture raising the hairs on the back of her neck. She tried not to flinch from Gregory's touch, plastered on a smile, and turned to face him. "Nice speech."

"Thank you, Vivian."

"Isn't Lauren annoyed you're passing her project off as your own?"

"She knows what's best." He reached into his jacket pocket and pulled out a white envelope, the same he did every year. "Here, this is for you. It's your bonus."

Vivian shook her head. "I don't want it." It felt too much like prostituting herself out to him. She felt dirty.

"I'm starting to feel like you no longer want to work here."

"What was your first clue?"

Gregory narrowed his eyes. He glanced to the left and right, then stepped even closer. "I'm losing my patience with you. Either smarten up or quit. I won't have my *employee* making a fool of me."

Vivian turned her head away from his whiskey breath, her gaze spotting Lauren heading out the exit. She stepped away from him. "Excuse me, I need the ladies' room." She pushed her way through the crowd, out the exit, and into the carpark. Lauren was nearing the back of the lot where Vivian assumed her car was. She sprinted after her, cursing the heels she wore. "Lauren," she called out. Lauren cocked her head

at hearing her name but didn't slow down. "Lauren, wait."
Lauren stopped and turned around just as Vivian reached her.
"What?"

"I, um." Now Vivian was face to face with her, she didn't
know what to say. She settled on pleasantries. "How are
you?"

"Just great."

"I didn't expect to see you here tonight."

"Couldn't miss the dog and pony show. Have a nice
evening."

Lauren began to turn but Vivian reached out, stopping
her. "Wait."

"I've got places to be."

Vivian dropped her hand. "I miss you."

"You don't get to say that to me. You were the one who
walked away, remember?"

"I know. I'm sorry. I had to."

"No, you didn't. You chose to."

"I did it for you."

Lauren laughed harshly, throwing her hands in the air.
"You don't get it, do you? I don't give a God damn about the
health club or the money I spent getting it started. I thought it
was what I wanted, but it wasn't. When my mum died, I was
lost. I had no focus. Then I met you and everything changed.
The idea for the spa came along. All this time, I thought that
was what I wanted, what I needed to make me whole again.
But it wasn't. What I needed was *you*. It was you who had
got me back on the right path after that first meeting a year
ago. When we were in Scotland, I was so happy. I fell in love
with you, and you walked away."

Vivian was dismayed to see tears streaming down Lauren's face. Vivian's hands shook, her legs feeling like they wanted to give out. "I thought it was the right thing to do. I didn't want your father to take away the funding."

"So instead you came back here to work for him?" Lauren scrubbed a hand across her face, wiping the tears away, and leaned in a little closer. "Tell me, Vivian, has he got you into bed yet?"

Vivian's hand shot out before she could stop herself. "How dare you! These past two months have been unbearable for me. Working beside him, watching him leer at me, and all because I wanted you to have your dream."

"*You* were my dream. And he took you away just like I said he would. You broke my heart. There's no coming back from that."

"If that's all true, then why didn't you follow me back here? Fight for me? You stayed up there and finished the project. Don't tell me I was all you wanted, because I clearly wasn't."

Lauren straightened and took a breath. In a calm voice, she said, "You should find Damien."

"What? Why?"

"Ask him about his visit to me earlier this month."

Vivian shook her head, not understanding. "What are you talking about?"

"Find him and ask him. Then you will know what it was I wanted. Goodnight, Vivian."

With that, Lauren turned and stalked away to her car. Vivian watched until the car was no longer in sight, then headed back into the building. She searched for twenty minutes, avoiding Gregory, before she spotted Damien in a small group by the bar. She grasped his forearm.

"Damien, can I have a moment, please?"

Damien glanced at her. "Of course." He looked back at the group. "Excuse me." He followed Vivian out into the same corridor where Vivian had first met Lauren. Her skin flushed as memories of that night surfaced. "What can I do for you, Vivian?"

"I need to ask you something about Lauren."

"Lauren? She's around here somewhere. You can talk to her yourself."

"I've already spoken to her. She told me to ask you about your recent visit up there."

Damien furrowed his brow, shrugging his shoulders at the same time. "I went to invite her to the party and check out the health club."

"No, it's more than that."

"What's going on?" His eyes narrowed. "What I discussed with my sister is no one's business, not yet anyway. Why would she get you to ask me about it?"

Vivian didn't speak for a moment, hesitant to reveal her true relationship with Lauren. However, if she wanted to find out what was going on, she didn't have a choice. She took a breath. "While we were up there, we became...lovers."

"Ah, now it makes sense." Damien grinned.

"What does?"

"After she showed me around the health club, we went for a drink. I wanted to tell her about my new business venture I was thinking about. She told me she had a better idea. She offered me the spa."

"What?" To say Vivian was stunned would be an understatement. The health club was everything Lauren had wanted. For her to give it up something big must have happened. *It did, we fell in love.*

"She said that the reason she was building it was no longer valid, that her heart wasn't in it anymore. She was tired of dealing with Dad, of him having financial control over it all. She wanted out. I pressed her on the issue and asked what had changed."

"What did she tell you?"

He shrugged again. "She said Dad had taken something special from her, and being up there only brought her heartache."

"Oh, God." Vivian's hands went to her stomach, fearing she'd throw up. Leaving had been the biggest mistake of her life. It was clear now that Lauren only wanted her. The realisation should have brought her immense pleasure but it didn't. *I walked out on her.* All she had done was break both their hearts. Lauren was right, there was no coming back from that.

"I asked her to elaborate, but she wouldn't. She just wanted out."

"So, if she signed it over to you, why is she still up there?"

"She wanted to prove to Dad that she has what it takes to be the best, like him. She has no interest in *being* like him but wanted him to know she shouldn't be treated the way she has been. She wanted him to know she is smarter than he thinks, that she's worthy, or some such nonsense. I know they've never gotten along. I don't know what his problem is with her, but I guess this was her way of sticking him the middle finger." He tilted his head down, gazing at her from under his long lashes. "Am I right to assume the something special he took from her was you?"

"Yes. He told me if I didn't come back here with him, he'd pull the funding and she wouldn't be able to complete the build."

Damien shook his head. "So you left thinking the spa was what she wanted?"

"Yes."

"But what she wanted was you?"

"Yes."

"Did she tell you that?"

Vivian nodded, her gut sinking further. "Yes, the day I left."

"And you didn't believe her?"

He sounded incredulous, as he should be. Lauren had never lied to her. Vivian should have stayed and talked it out with her instead of assuming she knew what was best for them both.

"I thought I was doing the right thing."

"What will you do now?"

"There's nothing I can do." Tears formed in her eyes. "She wants nothing to do with me."

"Do you want my advice?"

"Couldn't hurt."

"Quit."

She shook her head vigorously. "I can't."

"You can. You have no obligation to my father. Come May first, he'll no longer have any financial input into the business. I've secured all the necessary loans to buy him out."

"But they signed a contract."

"Yes. That Gregory will have a stake in the business until such time Lauren can pay him back. That's what I'll be doing on the first. If you quit and he pulls the remaining funds, it won't matter. The project is virtually finished, and I have enough funds to do the opening ceremony. His money means nothing anymore."

"Regardless, Lauren won't want to see me."

"You won't know unless you try."

Could she leave Bridger Holdings and go after Lauren? There was no deciding, she knew what she would do. She couldn't stomach working for Gregory any longer. Even if Lauren refused to see her, she still wouldn't want to work for him. Especially after the way he had treated them both.

"You're right. Thanks, Damien."

"No problem. I'm just glad my sister has finally fallen in love."

"Let's hope she's willing to forgive me."

"You did nothing wrong. You just wanted to do what was best."

"Thanks." She was pleased he didn't hold any ill will toward her. If things did work out with Lauren, he would be her brother-in-law. He was a nice guy. She could see why Lauren was hesitant to tell him about their mother's affair.

"Do you know where she's staying?"

"With me and my family. Here's the address." He reached into his pocket, pulling out a business card and a pen. Vivian glanced at it, wondering what type of person always had a pen on them. Damien must have caught her look because he said, "My dad taught me you should never leave home without a pen and business cards. You never know if you might meet a future business associate. He was right." He scribbled on the back of the card and handed it to Vivian.

"You don't mind if I turn up there?"

"No. The kids and my wife are with my wife's parents for the night, so Lauren will be there by herself."

"Okay, thank you, Damien." She stepped forward and hugged him tightly. "You're a great brother." She stepped back and Damien cleared his throat.

"Come to the opening. I'll reserve you a front-row ticket."

"Will do." She smiled and made a hasty retreat to her car. Thirty minutes later, she pulled up to Damien's large house. Her eyes went wide at the size of the building. She knew he had money but had no idea how much. It was nearly the size of Gregory's. The contrast between what Damien and Gregory had compared to Lauren was no more apparent than now. Lauren practically had nothing. Vivian knew she had sold everything she could to raise funds for the build. By Vivian's reckoning, Lauren was now technically homeless. Especially now she had signed the health club over to Damien. *She gave up everything for me.* Vivian had to swallow a few times to hold back the urge to wail. *How could I have been so stupid?* There was no time for questions, she needed to find Lauren.

She stepped from her car, noting no lights were on in the house. Lauren's car was not in the driveway. With a sinking feeling she was too late, she walked up the long pathway. She knocked and rang the bell for ten minutes with no sign of Lauren. *I've missed her, she's gone.* Not caring that she didn't belong on the property, she sank to the floor, leaned back against the door, and cried.

†

Vivian wasn't sure how long she'd sat there before headlights illuminated her. She glanced up, recognising Gregory's car. Another car pulled in behind him and they both rolled to a stop. Damien emerged from the second car and rushed over to her. He put his arm around her shoulders and helped her stand. Vivian wiped the tears away from her face, embarrassed she had been caught crying.

"Vivian, are you okay?"

"She's gone." Vivian looked up into Damien's confused gaze, paying no attention to Gregory who stood a few feet away.

"What?"

"She isn't here. I was too late."

"Come here."

Damien wrapped his other arm around her. Vivian nestled her head into his chest, his cologne similar to the one her father used to wear. For a moment, she wished Duncan was alive and able to console her. Damien smoothed her back, she squeezed him a little tighter.

"What's going on?" Gregory's voice sounded impatient. "Vivian, why are you here?"

Damien released her. She turned to Gregory, not caring tears still ran freely down her cheeks. "I wanted to see Lauren."

"I've had enough of this." Even in the dark of the night, Vivian could see his cheeks turning red. He heaved a huge sigh, his cheeks puffing out. "How many times—"

"I love her. She loves me, too."

"Don't be ridiculous."

"What's ridiculous is the way you've tried to control her." Vivian took a few steps forward, bringing her within touching distance of Gregory. Standing on the steps, she was now the same height as him, and it gave her a sense of control. "Do you have any idea how much hurt you've caused her over the years? How could you do that to your daughter?"

"She isn't mine. Why would I care how she feels?"

"What?" Damien asked. He stood next to Vivian. "Dad, what are you talking about?"

"Your whore of a mother had an affair. Lauren is someone else's problem."

"You're lying." Damien shook his head, biting his lip. Vivian wanted to comfort him but didn't know how. Hands on hips, he started to pace, head hanging low. She couldn't believe Gregory had blurted it out after all this time.

"Why do you think I've wanted nothing to do with her? She's a bastard."

Damien stopped pacing and stepped up to Gregory. "Don't ever call her that again."

"Why? What are you going to do about it, boy?" Gregory smirked. Vivian didn't have time to reach Damien before he pulled his fist back and punched Gregory square in the face. Gregory flew back, landing on his ass. Blood trickled from his nose. His eyes were wide as if he never thought Damien would hit him.

"You are a nasty piece of work," Damien seethed. "No wonder she signed the health club over to me."

"She can't do that."

"She can do whatever she likes. And in two weeks, you'll have your money back. Neither one of us wants anything to do with you." Damien turned his back on Gregory and took Vivian's hand, leading her back up the steps toward the front door. She heard Gregory get to his feet.

"You don't mean that. You're my son, my heir."

Damien stopped and glanced over his shoulder. "I don't want anything from you. You disgust me. Come on, Vivian. Let's go inside."

Damien unlocked the door and opened it wide. Before stepping through, Vivian glanced over to Gregory and said, "Oh, by the way, I quit."

"You will all rue the day you messed with me."

Damien slammed the door on Gregory and switched on the lights. He kept hold of Vivian's hand as he led her into the study. Vivian glanced around the room. It wasn't your typical home office. Although tall bookcases lined the walls, no books were present. On the shelves were trinkets and photographs. Model boats took up one bookcase all to themselves. Damien's love of the sea was obvious. Vivian sat on a velvet loveseat in the corner, her hands shaking as the adrenalin left her body. She didn't think the situation could get any worse, but it had. Lauren had never wanted Damien to find out the truth about their mother's affair. If Lauren found out it was because Vivian provoked Gregory, she would never forgive her.

Damien opened a cabinet and pulled out a bottle of whiskey and two glasses. He poured equal amounts into each and passed one over to Vivian. "Here."

"Thank you."

Vivian took a sip, as he pulled his phone from his pocket. He lifted it to his ear and waited. After a few moments, he tossed it down onto his desk. "I can't get hold of Lauren. It goes straight to voicemail." He settled a hip on the edge of the desk and ran a hand through his hair. He eyed Vivian. "So, is it true? Mum had an affair."

"I think you should talk to Lauren about this."

"She's not here. You are. Please, Vivian, tell me."

Going against her better judgment, Vivian started to speak. "According to Lauren, your mother met a man named Peter at the supermarket. They struck up a friendship, and yes, had an affair. When she fell pregnant, she ended it. Lauren doesn't think Peter knows about her. Your mother said she never told him."

"How did Dad find out?"

"When she asked for the divorce. She wanted to take you both with her to France, but he wouldn't allow it. She told him about Lauren, and he threw them both out."

"I always did wonder why she didn't take me with her." For a moment, Damien looked hurt. Vivian assumed he was reliving the moment he found out his mother wouldn't be taking him with her to France. He must have been so confused as a teenager, probably felt unwanted by her too. There was so much upset and lies within the Bridger family. Vivian wondered how any of them survived as well as they had.

"It also explains why Dad always shunned Lauren." He sipped his drink. "When did Lauren find out?"

"About five years ago, when your mother became ill."

"Why didn't she tell me?" The wounded look flashed across his features again.

"I think she thought you wouldn't see her as your sister anymore. You are the only family she has left, and she didn't want to lose you."

"What's going on?"

Vivian's gaze flew to the entrance of the study. Lauren stood before them, her eyes mere slits, lips set in a thin line. Anger rolled off her in waves. "Lauren! You're back."

"My flight got cancelled."

"You were leaving?" Damien asked.

"Yes." Lauren didn't explain any further. She pinned Vivian with a glare. "Now, care to explain what you're doing here and what you're talking about?"

Damien put his glass down and approached Lauren. "I know about Mum, about the affair."

Lauren kept her gaze fixed on Vivian. "You told him? How could you?"

"Let me explain."

"No. Get out. You had no right."

Vivian got to her feet, placing her glass onto the carpeted floor. She rushed over to her. "Lauren, a lot has happened in the last two hours."

"I don't care. Get out." Lauren turned and marched out of the room.

"It's okay, Vivian, I'll talk to her."

Vivian wanted to argue with him. She wanted to stay, to talk to Lauren. To try and explain everything that had happened. But it would do no good. She had never seen Lauren look so hurt before, not even when Vivian had left Scotland. Vivian's plan to come here and reconcile with her was dead in the water. She'd be lucky if Lauren ever spoke to her again. She nodded at Damien and headed for the front door. Lauren was sat on the stairs, head in her hands. "Please don't go until we talk."

Lauren didn't look up as she said, "Goodnight, Vivian."

"Goodnight." Damien walked Vivian out into the night. The spring night chilled Vivian's skin. She wrapped her arms around herself and turned to Damien. "Thank you, Damien, for everything."

"You're welcome." He hugged her quickly and kissed her cheek. "I'll see you at the opening."

Vivian nodded but couldn't bring herself to agree out loud. She didn't know if Lauren would be there. If Lauren refused to speak to her before then, there would be no point in going back up to Scotland. Deep down, she knew it was over between them. She just had to accept it. She climbed into her car and headed home. It was time to think about her future. She had no job and no Lauren. *It's Lesley all over again.* She had promised herself she would never let her love life interfere with her career. She had failed. *When will you learn?* At forty-one, she should have been able to keep control over every aspect of her life. She realised now how little control she had. *Maybe it's time I move. Start afresh. Lauren won't talk to me. I'm not going back to Bridger Holdings. What's keeping me here?*

There was nothing, not even a cat.

†

"Why didn't you tell me?" Damien sat down beside Lauren on the stairs.

"It doesn't matter." Lauren didn't lift her head from her hands. She couldn't face him. She had spent five years keeping this from him and now he knew. *God damn Vivian for doing this to me.* Lauren had been shocked to hear Vivian's voice coming from Damien's study. She hadn't expected to see her again. She had planned to fly back to Scotland, collect her things, and catch the next flight back to France. It had been her only thought after seeing Vivian at the party. She hurt so bad that even being in the same country as her was torture. Lauren had nothing left. Going back to the place she'd called home for most of her life seemed her only recourse. The plan was temporarily put on hold due to the cancelled flight. One night wouldn't matter. She would catch one tomorrow and be in France in two days. She wasn't sure she could do that now. Not now Damien knew the truth. She would need to stay for him. Lauren had always been able to read Damien. It wasn't hard to hear the heartbreak in his voice.

"Of course it matters. Lauren, I could have been there for you. Why didn't Dad ever say anything?"

"I don't think he knows I know." She lifted her head and glanced at him. "I have no idea why he never brought it up, or why he continued to allow me to be a part of the family."

"You *are* a part of the family."

Lauren shook her head. "No, I'm not. I'm the black sheep at all the gatherings. He uses my presence to pretend he's a wonderful father. I think he wanted everyone to know how perfect his life was, despite the divorce. You know how important appearances are to him."

"You could have told me. I could have helped you."

"Damien, we were never that close, not after Mother and I left." Lauren stood and took a few steps away. She needed the distance. She didn't want to cry in front of him. Sitting next to him only served to loosen her resolve on leaving. She kept her back to him as she spoke. "After Mum died, I came home and you were the only one who still wanted anything to do with me. I thought if you knew, you'd pull away from me. I couldn't lose you too." Her shoulders shook as the tears came. She lowered her head and pressed her fingers into her eyes, trying to stem the flow.

"You're an idiot." Damien took her arm and turned her. "You're my sister and I love you."

"I'm sorry."

"No, I'm sorry. I should have dug a little more into why he treated you so badly. If it makes you feel any better, I punched him tonight."

"What?" Lauren's head shot up, not sure she had heard right. By the satisfied smile on Damien's face, she had. "Why?"

"We left the party early, because he wanted to discuss his plans for opening an office in Australia. When we got here, Vivian was on the stoop, crying. She came here looking for you. She must have sat there for over an hour. Things got heated. She called him out for being cruel to you. He blurted out you weren't his, called you a name, so I hit him. I told him about you signing the spa over to me. He wasn't best pleased with that."

Vivian stood up for me. She wasn't the one who told Damien... It was Dad. A flow of guilt washed over Lauren for having blamed Vivian. *She waited for me.* The knowledge Vivian had come to see her and waited so long, crying, only strengthened her guilt.

"That's that then. I have no more ties to him. I'm free."

Damien nodded, smiling before his forehead creased as he frowned. "Why did you use his money if you knew he wasn't your real dad?"

"He was my last resort. At the time, I thought building the health club was what I needed to get my life on track. Using his money was the only way I could do it." Not that it mattered anymore. After all her hard work, the spa was no longer hers. She had wasted nearly five months building a project she had no interest in. *No, it wasn't a waste. Vivian and I became lovers. Even though it's over, I will never regret spending that time with her.*

"But the club isn't what you need, is it?" Damien ducked his head, catching Lauren's gaze with his own.

"I didn't realise it then, but I fell in love with her the first time I met her. Last year, at the party, I was making a dick of myself. She pulled me away to stop any embarrassment toward Dad. We talked a little and I kissed her. We connected that night, but I thought I wouldn't see her again. Then Dad insisted she come to keep an eye on me in Scotland. I don't think he trusted me not to run off with his money."

"And you two became close."

Lauren nodded. "We did. It was so amazing, being up there with her. But then Dad arrived and Vivian left. I was

171

heartbroken she could walk away like that. After she went, I lost all desire to keep going with the spa."

"You could have told me all that when I came up there."

"What was the point?" She lifted her arms as she shrugged. "She was gone, and I wanted out. You're not mad, are you?"

"No. The health club is amazing. I see no reason why it won't be a success. We could run it together."

"Thanks for the offer, but I don't think so. Too many memories."

"So what now?"

"So now I wait for a new flight to France."

"You can't seriously leave?" He sounded incredulous. "What about Vivian?"

"What about her?"

"She loves you. She quit her job tonight. She came here to work things out with you."

She quit. Lauren thought Vivian would never have the strength to walk away from Gregory, the expert manipulator. Lauren was sure Vivian would never get out from under him. *She deserves more credit than I'm giving her. She's always been strong, independent. That's what drew me to her in the first place.* "It's too late. There's too much pain involved now. I don't know if I can trust her again."

"Bullshit. Just talk to her."

In her heart of hearts, Lauren knew she wouldn't be able to leave without talking to Vivian. They needed to clear the air, sort through all the misunderstandings and heartache. *Maybe then we can both move on.* "I need time."

"Come to the opening. Dad won't be there, so you won't have to see him."

"I don't know." Lauren chewed her lip, instinctively knowing Vivian would be there. She wasn't sure two weeks would be enough time to gather the strength to talk to her without breaking down.

"Please. You should be there to see the end result, to see what you achieved."

Damien looked so earnest that Lauren found herself agreeing. She would go to the opening, talk with Vivian if she was there, then get a flight to France. It was time to start again.

"Okay. But after that, I'm leaving."

173

CHAPTER FOURTEEN

Vivian startled awake. Someone was knocking on the door. She glanced around, finding herself sprawled on the couch, wearing last night's dress. An empty wine bottle stood next to her open laptop, the screen still displaying LinkedIn. She had stayed up till God knows when searching for a new direction for her life. She had read openings for everything from local jobs to abroad. Nothing had caught her interest. Her thoughts always came back to Lauren. The knock sounded again. Vivian got to her feet and padded to the door. Annie stood on the other side, her bright smile turning into a frown as she looked Vivian up and down.

"Are you all right?"

Vivian sighed and stepped back from the threshold, allowing Annie to enter. "Not great. What can I do for you?"

"I'm supposed to be here for coffee." Annie's brows pinched together. "You obviously had a good evening. Too much to drink at the party?"

"No, too much back home." Vivian closed the door and went to the kitchen, Annie following behind her. "Take a seat. I'll get the coffee ready." She reached for the kettle, her eyes tearing. She bit her lip to stop the sobs coming out. She felt Annie's hand on her shoulder, turning her around.

"What's going on, Viv?"

"Lauren came to the party. I tried to talk to her, but she wasn't interested. It's over."

"Oh, honey."

Annie pulled her into her arms, hugging her tightly. Vivian held on and cried. Annie knew all about the situation in Scotland. Over the weeks, Annie had been a great sounding board. Vivian had ignored Annie's advice to go back to Scotland, to win Lauren back. Vivian had been too stubborn. She didn't want to risk Lauren losing the health club. Had she known then that Lauren wasn't interested in the club anymore, she would have driven back up there right away. She had missed her chance. Lauren was furious with her. Especially after telling Damien about their mother's affair.

"She hates me," Vivian mumbled into Annie's shoulder.

"I doubt that's true. She's probably still hurt you left. Give it time. She'll come around."

Vivian pulled back, glaring at Annie. "You didn't see her last night. Her eyes were filled with such anger. And now she's leaving. She gave up the spa. She was going to leave last night on a plane."

"Where to?"

"I don't know. All I do know is she won't want to ever see me again."

Annie took a breath. She reached up and wiped Vivian's tears away with her thumb. "Do you love her?"

"Of course."

"Then stop wallowing and do something to fix it. From what you told me about your time together, it's clear you are meant to be. She's upset, sure, but you can't just give up."

"What am I supposed to do? She's blocked my number. I doubt she's still staying with her brother anymore." She flung her hands in the air, frustrated. "I have no idea where she is. How am I supposed to declare my love for her if I can't find her?"

Annie shook her head and shrugged. "I don't know, but you're a smart woman. I'm sure you'll figure it out."

Vivian turned her back and picked up the kettle, her thoughts jumbling together. She was grateful for Annie's silence, which allowed her to concentrate on making the coffee. She set two mugs onto the table and took a seat, Annie taking the chair opposite her. They'd sat this same way many times before, as they caught up with each other's goings-on. They sipped in silence, Vivian staring at the tabletop.

"I guess my only hope is to go to the opening of the health club in a couple of weeks. Damien, that's Lauren's brother, did invite me up there. Hopefully, Lauren will be there."

"What if she's not?"

"Then it's over. For good." It wasn't a prospect Vivian relished, but she couldn't pine for Lauren forever. If Lauren refused to see her, there wasn't much else Vivian could do.

"Would you like me to come with you, for moral support?"

Vivian smiled. "Thank you, but I'll be fine." Her smile turned into a smirk. "I know you only want to come watch the drama unfold."

"Damn, you caught me." She clicked her fingers, grinning. "Seriously, though, if you need me to come, I will."

"Honestly, I'll be fine. If she isn't there, I'm sure I'll be back here soon enough, banging on your door for consoling."

Annie reached across the table and squeezed Vivian's forearm. "I'm here if you need me."

"Thank you. Now, tell me what you've been up to this week."

"Actually, can it wait? I was thinking you need a diversion from your troubles. Why don't you grab a shower and we can hit the shops. A little retail therapy is good for the soul."

Vivian had never been one to traipse around the shops looking for the latest fashions. Annie was right, though. It would do her no good sitting around all day mooning over Lauren. "That sounds great." She rose to her feet. "Are you sure you don't mind waiting while I get ready?"

"Of course not. I'll go home and grab my handbag and keys, and make sure Mike is okay with the kids for a few hours. Come on over when you're ready."

Vivian walked Annie to the door and gave her a quick hug. After Annie left, she went upstairs and stripped off her dress in the bathroom. She avoided looking at herself in the mirror, knowing how awful she looked. No doubt she had mascara streaks down her cheeks from all the crying. She turned on the shower and stepped in once it had warmed. Within minutes, she felt almost human. Once finished, she dressed and gave her teeth a good scrub. Her hair was still damp but she was fine to let it air dry. She was about to let herself out of the house, when her mobile buzzed in her pocket.

Meet me at HQ in half hour.

Gregory. Vivian stared at the message, her heart pounding. For a brief moment, she considered going to meet him. The thought of facing him turned her stomach, not that she was scared of him. She just didn't fancy having a showdown with him. She hit delete. Gregory Bridger was no longer any concern of hers. How Lauren and Damien tackled him was their problem. She was done being a part of his cruel game. She blocked his number, then slipped her phone back into her pocket. With any luck, that would be the end of it.

†

"Hey, Sis. What are you up to?"

Lauren turned her head to glance at Damien, who had just sat down next to her on the decking. It was early evening. The sun still hung in the sky, but Lauren was exhausted. The traumatic events had kept her awake most of the night. She wanted to see Vivian, to apologise for accusing her of telling Damien about their mother's affair.

She also wanted to kiss her. To feel her lips pressing into her own. She didn't know what was keeping her from doing just that. *You know why. She left.* The fact Vivian gave up on them so easily was the one thing stopping Lauren from finding her. *How could I trust her not to walk away again?* That was the crux of her issue. Lauren had been let down and hurt by too many people to fully put her trust in someone again. She sighed, her gaze finding Damien's son and daughter chasing each other over the back garden. "Just watching the kids playing."

"You not up for joining in?"

"I'm still stuffed from dinner. All that running around would probably kill me." Michelle, Damien's wife, had cooked a delicious lasagne. It was so nice that Lauren went back for seconds. Her appetite had been vacant since Vivian left Scotland, but one whiff of Michelle's cooking had her appetite returning full force.

"Probably." Damien grasped her shoulder. Lauren looked at him, eyebrows raised in question. "I want to thank you for sticking around an extra day."

"That's okay. It was nice to talk it all out with you. I have to go back up to Scotland tomorrow, make sure everything is still on schedule."

"I can't believe you were going to hop on a plane to France without seeing the build to its end."

"Terry has everything under control for the soft opening. It's just the finishing touches to do. I left him detailed instructions. And don't forget, I was planning on going back. It's just, after I saw Vivian at the party, I wanted to be as far away from her as possible." Leaving Terry to finish all the work wasn't the grown-up thing to do, but last night she

179

hadn't cared. Her sense of duty returned with the new day. She would go back, finish the project for Damien, then be on her way. If she could do all that without seeing Vivian, she'd be happy. *You're lying to yourself. Just talk to her.*

"Well, I'm glad you're going to finish the project and stay for the opening. You are still staying, right?"

"Yes. I'll be there for the opening, but I'm not sure what I'll say to Vivian if she accepts your invitation."

Damien shrugged a shoulder, the corner of his lip pulling up. "You could go and see her now. I'm sure I can find her address out for you."

"No." Lauren shook her head. "I'm not ready."

"And you think two weeks stewing about it will prepare you any better?"

"Probably not, but one can hope." *Maybe by then, I'll have a handle on my thoughts and emotions.* All the back and forth, warring within herself, was driving her crazy.

"I'm sorry this has all been so shit for you. Not just Vivian. Dealing with Mum's illness, Dad being a prick to you, everything." Damien lowered his head, catching Lauren's gaze. "I promise, I'll always be here for you if you need me."

"Thank you."

The doorbell chimed, startling them both. "Who do you think that is?"

"I'll give you one guess." Lauren was surprised their father hadn't already made an appearance. From what Damien said, Gregory was furious he would no longer be part of the health club. Knowing her father, she didn't expect him to go away quietly. Lauren got to her feet and held out her hand to help Damien up. "I'll go let him in. You might want to ask Michelle to take the kids out for a bit."

"Good idea. I'll see you in there."

Lauren nodded, then headed through the house. She took a few deep breaths before opening the front door. Gregory looked as smart as always, dressed in a dark, blue suit. The only abnormality was the bruise on his jawline and slight swelling to his nose. Lauren had to stop herself from smiling, knowing Damien had put it there. She was slightly pissed off she hadn't witnessed the punch. She had waited a long time for someone to put Gregory in his place.

"Hi, Dad."

"You're still here?"

"Just until tomorrow." Lauren ignored his smile of pleasure at hearing she would be gone soon. She idly thought about adding another bruise to the opposite side of his face. *Things always look better when they match.*

"Where's Damien?"

"He's going to meet us in the study in a minute. Come on through." She stepped back and allowed him entry but couldn't resist a snarky comment as he passed her by. "Your face looks painful."

"I've had worse."

"That doesn't surprise me." She followed him into the study, closing the door behind her.

"You've always been insolent."

"And you've always been a hate-filled old man."

"How dare you speak to me that way." Gregory's face went red. The vein on his temple throbbed. He ground out the words through gritted teeth.

181

"I'll speak to you however I damn well please. It's not like you're my father, is it?"

Gregory's eyes went wide for a moment but then relaxed. He glanced away. "Damien told you then?"

"No. I've known since Mum got sick."

"You knew all this time and you didn't say anything?"

"You've known since I was eleven and never told me."

"I was trying to protect you."

"Bullshit," Lauren shouted. She wasn't going to let him get away with the lie. He had never done anything for anyone, only himself. "You were protecting yourself. You didn't want people to know you couldn't keep your wife happy."

"So you *were* trying to get at my money?"

"Is that all you care about?" *We're talking about you not being my father and all you can think is that I was after your money?* "I can't believe this." Lauren ignored his question, wanting to tell him exactly how she'd felt over the years. "I never said anything because you were still my dad and I was under the stupid illusion we could have a relationship." She glared at him. He stood unflinching. "But you never liked me, did you? You could never get past the fact I wasn't yours. I tried everything to please you, but you didn't care. You may not have been my biological father, but you were my *dad*. I was just a kid. You threw me out without a second thought. Like I was some piece of trash. How could you do that?"

"I would like to know that, too," Damien said from the doorway. Lauren hadn't heard him enter, too caught up in her tirade. She was pleased for his presence. Damien strode across the study and stood next to Lauren. He smiled quickly at her.

"This doesn't concern you, Damien." Gregory's gaze narrowed ever so slightly.

"Yes, it does. Lauren is my sister. You didn't have to treat her the way you did."

"I didn't know how to deal with it. I was so in love with your mother. We were the perfect match. To find out she cheated on me and had a child with some runt... That broke my heart. You were my little girl, and she took you away from me."

For a moment, Gregory looked almost sad. Lauren nearly felt sorry for him, but she pushed it aside. He didn't deserve her sorrow. Not that she believed his words. If Gregory cared about her that much growing up, he wouldn't have let their relationship dwindle, no matter how far away she lived.

"No, she didn't. Just because we were no longer blood-related, that shouldn't have erased the years you spent bringing me up. For years, I wondered what I had done wrong, why you no longer treated me the same. I thought there was something wrong with me. Turns out it was because you felt emasculated." Lauren's eyes filled with tears. She didn't bother to wipe them away. "It was never anything to do with me."

Gregory waved his hand in the air as if brushing away Lauren's words like they meant nothing. "I didn't come here to talk about all this. I want to know what's going on with the health club. Why did you sign it over to Damien?"

"Are you serious right now?" Damien bellowed. "Lauren is devastated, and you want to talk about business?"

Lauren grabbed Damien's arm, pulling him back from advancing on Gregory. By the look in his eyes, he wanted to thump him again. "Damien, it's okay. It's what I expect from him." She turned her attention back to Gregory. "I signed it over because I no longer want anything to do with it. My reason is none of your business. You'll have every penny back in two weeks. You no longer have to worry if I'm out for your money." Gregory huffed, obviously displeased with her answer. "Also, the moment you leave, you won't ever hear from me again."

"The contract stated I would be getting a share of the profits. I should be compensated."

Not even a flicker of emotion at never seeing me again. Lauren wasn't surprised. "You really are a greedy asshole. Read the contract. It was profits until such time I pay you back. There are no profits, because you're being paid back in thirteen days. Before we open."

"You should go now, Dad," Damien said.

"I can't believe you did this behind my back. You're my son and heir."

"I don't want to be your heir. And quite frankly, I don't want to be your son, either."

For the first time since arriving, Gregory looked frantic. His eyes widened, forehead creasing. Lauren could see his hands shake. It was the first time Lauren had ever seen him lose his composure.

"You don't mean that," Gregory begged, sweat beading in his hairline. "Come on, Damien. This is all just emotional twaddle. Don't let Lauren's tears fool you into thinking I'm some kind of monster."

"Lauren didn't do this, you did. Now, please leave my home or I'll have you arrested for trespassing."

Gregory stared at them both, his lips set in a thin line. Lauren stood with her back straight, Damien by her side. She took Damien's hand. Together they made a united front. This would be the last time she would see Gregory. She wanted to make it clear he no longer had any power over her.

She was free.

"Fine. If the money isn't in my account by close of business in thirteen days, I'll be suing you both."

With that, Gregory stormed from the study. The slamming of the front door vibrated through the walls. Lauren let out a deep breath, her shoulders dropping. She let go of Damien's hand. It was over.

"Are you okay?" Damien asked.

"Yes. It's not the way I would have liked the conversation to have gone down, but I'm glad I got to say my piece. That's been building up for years." She felt thirty pounds lighter. She kicked herself for not having it out with him sooner. She didn't get the response she wanted from Gregory. She had hoped once she told him how she felt he would apologise, maybe hug her and promise to do better. It was a stupid fantasy. All he cared about was money. *And Damien. Why couldn't he ever feel that way about me?* It was a question she would never get an answer for. It was time to let it go.

"I'm so sorry."

"Please, you don't need to apologise. This is his doing. You don't have to end your relationship with him because of me."

"You're kidding, right? Lauren, he's despicable. I don't want someone like that around my family, and that includes you."

Lauren beamed at him. All her worry Damien would not see her as his sister, turns out, was unfounded. She wrapped her arms around his waist and squeezed tightly. "I love you."

"Me too." Damien pulled back and ruffled her hair. "How about we open the rum and discuss the opening? Michelle won't be back for a little while. She's taken the kids to the park and to get ice cream."

"Sounds great. I've got some information on the laptop you'll want to look at, so you'll have an idea of the running order." Although Lauren would now be present for the soft opening, she thought it best if Damien knew what to expect. She hoped she could talk him into doing the speech. It was going to be his business from now on anyway. It would be best if the staff and prospective clients saw him as the boss.

CHAPTER FIFTEEN

Lauren stood at the back of the fitness studio, her gaze scanning the crowd. It was a good turnout. Almost all of the people she had invited had come. Everyone was dressed in their finest clothes. She smiled to herself, pleased she had remembered to install a temporary floorcovering and protect the hardwood underneath from the women's high heels. The champagne flowed and hors d'oeuvres were served by a three-person waitstaff. The gathering in the fitness studio would last for a half hour before Damien gave his speech. After that, the guests would be free to roam the club and grounds as they wished. Damien was right. It felt good be there and witness this final stage. She would have been filled with regret had she missed it.

"Good crowd."

Lauren turned to find Damien beside her. He looked handsome in his tux, although nervous. He kept fidgeting with his tie. "Yes. Fingers crossed most want to take on membership." She reached up and stilled his hand. "Would you stop that? You look fine."

"Easy for you to say. You don't have to get up there and talk."

Lauren laughed. "Damien, you've done speeches, pitches, and boardroom meetings a million times. Why are you freaking out?"

"I just want it to go well."

"Everything will be fine."

"I still think you should do it."

Lauren shook her head. "This is your place now. People need to see your face up there, to know who the boss is."

"Yeah, I guess you're right." He didn't look convinced. "I forgot to tell you. The funds have been sent over to Dad. That should make him happy."

"Good."

"Have you heard from him at all?"

"No. And I don't expect to. Although, I am surprised he hasn't shown up here."

"I told Elliot not to admit anyone who is not on the guest list, including Dad."

"Perfect." The last thing she wanted was him showing up and making a scene. She hadn't heard from him since he left Damien's two weeks ago, which was fine by her. She wasn't happy Damien still refused to talk to him. They had always been close, but Damien reassured her it was what he wanted. *I'd pick you over Dad any day of the week.* The memory of that conversation started a little happy dance in her belly, knowing her brother loved her so much.

"Is the staff all in place? Once the speech is over, I want everyone to start exploring."

"Yes. Frankie, from the agency, has got that all sorted." The team members were scattered about the spa, ready to show guests around and answer any questions they had. They were yet to find a fulltime manager, but all the other staff had been interviewed and trained by Frankie. Damien had asked Lauren to stay until the manager was found, but she declined. Her flight to France was the next morning. Damien understood her wanting to leave, but that didn't stop him asking every five minutes if she'd reconsider.

"I'd better get up there."

"Good luck."

Damien smiled brightly and kissed her cheek. Lauren watched, as he stood on the makeshift stage and tapped the microphone. The din of the crowd quieted, all eyes on him.

"Ladies and gentlemen. I want to thank you all for coming out here today. You are the first to see the amazing amount of work that has gone into getting this place up and running. I'm confident that once you walk around and see what we have to offer, you'll be signing up before you leave. For those of you that do sign up today, you'll get unlimited access to all the amenities for the next month until the official opening. That offer also extends to your family members and friends.

"These past months, my sister, Lauren, has worked her butt off to get the health club up to the standard you see before you. She has a tremendous eye for detail. She and her crew have done an amazing job." Damien looked over at

189

Lauren. "I'm proud of you, Lauren." A round of cheers from the crowd sounded out. "Again, thank you all for coming. Help yourself to food and drinks, but be careful by the pool. I don't want any accidents." The crowd laughed along with him. "Now, let's all raise a glass and toast the opening of Celeste's."

Lauren raised her glass, a tear forming in her eye. She had debated over the name for weeks. Everything she came up with sounded cheesy or lame. Vivian had been the one to suggest she use her mother's name. As soon as Vivian said it, Lauren knew it would be perfect. It was the ultimate way to keep her mother's memory alive. If Damien decided to go ahead with a chain of clubs, Celeste's name would be known all around the country. It was a fitting end to this chapter in Lauren's life.

The doors opened, and the crowd began to file out. Within a few minutes, only Lauren remained. She turned around to put her glass on the table, her intention to mingle with the guests. A movement by the door caught her attention.

A vision of beauty stood twenty feet away. One shoulder proudly bared itself from the midnight-blue dress. Shining tresses were swept into a high, loose bun before cascading down and over the other shoulder. The woman's small clutch matched her dress. She smiled nervously. Lauren blinked; not sure she was real.

She hadn't seen or heard from Vivian in two weeks, not since the night at Damien's. Lauren had a feeling she would show up today but hadn't noticed her in the crowd. *Maybe she just arrived.* She tried to make her feet move, but they wouldn't comply. Rooted in place, Lauren watched Vivian's smile dim. Damien had been right, a two-week wait to see her hadn't made it any easier to come up with something to say. Vivian's shoulders dropped. She looked away, then turned and took a step toward the door. *She's leaving!* Lauren dropped the glass onto the table, not caring it landed on its side, spilling champagne. She raced after Vivian. She grabbed her shoulder and spun her around.

Up close, Lauren couldn't help but be captivated by Vivian's eyes and her perfume tickling her nostrils. The last few months fell away. All of Lauren's hurt drifted into the recesses of her mind. All that mattered was Vivian, standing before her, chest rising and falling with her rapid breathing.

"You came," Lauren murmured.

"I wouldn't miss the big opening. Congratulations, Lauren. The place looks wonderful."

"*You* look wonderful," Lauren corrected. Vivian blushed, her head dipping. Lauren cupped Vivian's cheek, raising her chin to catch her gaze again. "Come with me."

"Where?"

"To the cottage."

Vivian shook her head. "What about the event?"

"I don't care about the event. I need to be with you without all these people around." She stared at Vivian's lower lip pulled between between perfect teeth, then let her eyes plead her case. "Please."

"Okay."

Lauren smiled widely and took Vivian's hand. She led her through the building and to the carpark, luckily avoiding everyone. They settled into Lauren's car, and she sped away with a spray of gravel. She didn't know what she was thinking. They had so much to talk about. But all Lauren wanted to do was get Vivian of her dress and make her come. It had been a long two and a half months. She couldn't wait any longer to have her.

Consequences be damned.

†

Lauren unlocked the front door with one hand while holding Vivian's in the other. She flung the door wide and pulled her inside, the door closing behind them. Lauren didn't stop walking until they were in Vivian's old room. She spun around. Mere inches away from Vivian, Lauren's nerves surfaced. She gazed down into Vivian's eyes, her body trembling.

"You look beautiful." Lauren raised her hand to run her fingers through the hair that flowed over Vivian's shoulder.

Vivian smiled, her skin flushing, then she glanced away. "What are we doing, Lauren?" She took a step back. "We should talk before we do anything."

"I don't want to talk. I want to kiss you." Lauren stepped forward and cupped Vivian's cheek. The warmth of her skin calmed Lauren. Vivian was right; they should talk, but it would have to wait. All Lauren wanted was to reconnect with her, to feel Vivian writhing beneath her. She lowered her head, feeling Vivian's breath coat her face. Vivian's eyes closed, lips parting, then her tongue peeked out to wet those lips. Lauren closed the gap and crushed her mouth to Vivian's. Vivian grasped Lauren's waist, as Lauren pressed into her, backing her up against the wall. *She tastes just as good as I remember.* Lauren found the clasp in Vivian's hair and pulled it free, allowing her to thread her fingers through the silky strands. She felt Vivian's hands working the button on her trousers. Lauren pulled her back an inch. "Are you sure?"

Vivian opened her eyes, her gaze scorching. "I've wanted this from the moment I left. Help me out of this dress."

Lauren kissed her quickly, then spun her around. She lowered the zipper, then the dress, watching it pool around Vivian's ankles. She was braless, the smooth skin on her back begging to be touched. Lauren let her hands roam free, sweeping up Vivian's sides, over her shoulders, and down the middle. She hooked her fingers in the waistband of Vivian's thong and lowered that also. Vivian attempted to turn around, but Lauren crushed her own body to Vivian's back, holding her against the wall.

"Stay there. I want you like this." Vivian nodded. Lauren smiled and kissed her neck. She wound her arms around Vivian, one hand finding her breast, the other snaking down to her centre. Vivian jerked as Lauren's fingers found her clit. "I've missed you so much." She dipped her fingers, feeling how wet Vivian was. "I never thought I would be hooked on someone as much as I am on you." Vivian began to move in time with Lauren's hand, her breaths coming in gasps. "I'll never get enough of you." She kissed her neck again, pumping her hand harder. Vivian cried out as her climax hit. With lightning reflexes, Vivian spun around and pushed Lauren away. Buttons flew from Lauren's shirt as Vivian ripped it open. She stripped Lauren of her trousers and underwear. She pushed her again, causing Lauren to fall back onto the bed.

"No one has ever turned me on like you do." Vivian's roaming gaze left Lauren feeling devoured. The weight of

Vivian's body pressed her securely to the mattress, before kisses began at her mouth and worked their way down her body. Vivian's mouth finally found Lauren's opening. She held on to the bedsheets, trying not to thrash around too much from Vivian's oral assault. Her orgasm built then exploded. She screwed her eyes shut, as wave after wave of spasms rocketed through her body. Lauren threaded her hand into Vivian's hair, pulling her up to lie next to her.

"You're amazing." Lauren panted, finding it hard to settle her breathing. Tears formed in Vivian's eyes. "What's wrong?"

Vivian shook her head slightly, then buried herself under Lauren's chin. "Nothing. I'm just so glad I'm here with you. I didn't think you'd want to see me."

Lauren took a deep breath and wrapped her arms around Vivian. "I haven't stopped thinking about you since the moment you left. Once I finally realised you weren't coming back, I tried to let you go. I couldn't do it though." She shifted so she could capture Vivian's gaze, wanting her to see how serious she was about them. "I was angry at you, and my stubbornness nearly destroyed everything. I don't ever want to lose you again."

"I'm so sorry for everything. I only did what I thought was right."

"Shush, it's okay. I know." Lauren kissed her quickly. "We both did things we regret. Let's just put it behind us and move on."

"Do you think it will be that easy?"

"As long as we're open and talk about things, then yeah, I do."

"Can we talk later?" Vivian rolled on top of Lauren, straddling her waist. "I'd rather continue devouring you for a while."

Lauren's lips quirked. "I can live with that."

Their lovemaking continued into the night, sometimes hot and passionate, other times slow and sensuous. More tears were shed, tears of happiness. Despite everything Gregory had done to break them apart, they had found each other again. Lauren was determined to keep it that way. She loved Vivian with every fibre of her being. She wasn't going to let her go again. Lauren knew they still needed to talk about the future. Vivian was out of a job, and she herself had no other plans except going to France. Did having Vivian back in her life mean she should stay in England? Probably. But until they talked and she found out what Vivian wanted, her life would be in limbo. She was okay with that. Vivian was with her and that was all that mattered.

†

Vivian opened her eyes and quickly shut them. Sunlight beamed in through the open curtains. She blinked a few times, as she adjusted to the light. She was on her side, hands curled under her chin. Lauren wasn't with her. Her heart pounded in her chest. *Is that all I get, one night?* She couldn't believe Lauren would leave, but the sheets were cool next to her. She rolled over, and took a deep breath, inhaling the scent of Lauren's perfume. Vivian would commit Lauren's scent memory, knowing she would never smell it again. *I can't believe she would leave.* Her eyes teared.

195

A loud noise came from the direction of the kitchen. Vivian threw off the covers. Not caring she was completely naked, she ran from the room. She skidded to a halt at the threshold. Lauren crouched by the island, sweeping coffee granules into a dustpan. She glanced up at Vivian.

"Sorry if I woke you. I dropped the damn coffee jar."

"I thought you'd left." Vivian swayed to the side, the relief at seeing Lauren overwhelming her. Lauren glanced up again. Her forehead creased. She must have sensed Vivian's distress, as she dropped the pan, and raced over. Vivian clung to her, tears falling free.

"No, never." Lauren smoothed Vivian's back. "How could you think that?"

Vivian pulled back and shrugged a shoulder, feeling foolish for assuming the worst. "The bed was empty."

"Vivian, I got up to make you breakfast in bed. There isn't much left here, but I managed to find some bread in the freezer and eggs. I would never leave without saying something."

"I should have known that, but I couldn't help thinking we would only have one night. I wouldn't blame you if you left, not after what I did."

Lauren shook her head and sighed. She stepped around Vivian and disappeared up the hallway. She came back a moment later carrying the shirt she'd worn the day before. She draped it over Vivian's shoulders, and Vivian threaded her arms through the sleeves. Lauren took her hand.

"Come, we need to talk." Vivian allowed Lauren to lead her to the lounge, where they settled side by side on the couch, Lauren never let go of Vivian's hand. "I'm sorry you thought I'd left. Next time, I'll make sure you're awake when I leave the bed."

"Next time?" A kernel of hope flared in Vivian's chest.

"Yes. Vivian, things have been tumultuous between us for the last few months. To be honest, I wasn't sure I'd ever see you again. I'm all set to fly out to France soon."

"You're leaving?"

"That was the plan. But then you showed up yesterday and all my plans dissipated." Lauren looked away for a moment. "I'm not sure what I'll do now. One thing we need to get straight is that I love you, and I want to be wherever you are. Damien is set to run the place up here. I'm officially no longer the owner. I'm free to go wherever I want, and what I want is to be with you."

Vivian smiled at Lauren's words. Lauren was willing to take a chance on her and that was the best feeling in the world. She still needed to apologise to her though. "I never should have left. I'm sorry I did. I never meant to hurt you. I thought it was the right thing to do."

"You need to stop apologising. You did nothing wrong. I know it was because you loved me that you thought you should go."

"I do love you, Lauren. More than you know."

"Then let's stop worrying about the things in the past and concentrate on the future. That's if you still want me?"

"I've never wanted anyone as much as I want you." Vivian inched her head forward and pressed her lips to Lauren's. She kept the kiss chaste, not wanting things to move too quickly before they had finished talking. They needed to clear the air about everything, and they couldn't do that if their passion overtook them. "I assume you know I no longer work for Gregory?"

Lauren nodded. "Damien told me. How do you feel about that?"

"Couldn't be happier. It was unbearable being there for the last two months. He wanted us to pretend to be a couple, to show the outside world how well he was doing." Lauren's eyes narrowed, clearly unhappy about his plan. "He said it would all be for show, that he had no interest in me, but it wasn't hard to see he hoped we would become an item."

"I feel sick just thinking about that."

"I knew then I would be leaving. He even threatened to pull your funding, but right then I didn't care. He made me feel dirty, like he could buy my affection with the promise of money."

"I'll kill him." Lauren's hands clenched into fists, her lips pressed into a tight line.

"Honey, it's fine." Vivian covered Lauren's hands with her own. "He can't hurt us anymore."

"I know, but still, he knew I loved you. Why does he have to take everything from me?"

"He'll never take me from you, not again. I love you."

"I love you." Lauren loosened her fists, entwining their fingers. "What will you do now?"

Vivian thought for a moment. She still hadn't been able to find a job that interested her. She wasn't in any hurry. Her savings would keep her comfortable for a while. All she wanted was to be with Lauren, to reacquaint themselves with each other without the threat of Gregory looming over them. "Are you sure you don't want to run Celeste's?"

"Positive. Maybe if Damien wants to expand in the future, I could help him with that. For now, I'm done with it. This year has sucked a lot of energy from me. I need time to rejuvenate."

"Then take me to France."

"What?"

"Take me to France. Show me where you grew up. I loved hearing the stories you told me about where you lived. I'd love to see it in person."

"Really?"

Vivian nodded, smiling widely. There was nothing keeping her there. She had her family, and Annie, but it wasn't like she would be gone for good. A couple of months alone with Lauren sounded like the perfect idea. "Nothing would bring me more joy."

"Okay." Lauren lunged toward Vivian, wrapping her arms around her.

Vivian cupped Lauren's cheeks, gazing in her eyes. "It's you and me now, forever."

"Just the two of us. I love you."

"I love you, Lauren."

They scrambled from the couch and rushed to the bedroom, tossing off clothing as they went. Vivian had never been happier. Lauren was right, the last few months had sucked a lot of her energy also. She couldn't wait to get her ticket booked and jet off to Lauren's hometown in France, with nothing but their love to guide them.

CHAPTER SIXTEEN

Seven months later...

"Merry Christmas, love."

Lauren glanced to the side, as Vivian's wrapped an arm around her neck from behind and rested her chin on Lauren's shoulder. "Happy Christmas." Vivian kissed Lauren's cheek, then moved around the armchair and settled in her lap. Lauren wrapped her arms around to keep Vivian from falling off. "What time is it?"

"About seven. Why are you up so early?"

Lauren looked away. Her vacant gaze found the window that overlooked a stream running through the hills. Snow was falling thick and heavy, obscuring everything from view. She hadn't realised how long she'd been sitting there with her thoughts spinning in many directions. They had been in France for seven months, with no plans to return to England. Vivian found a job working for a hotel in Paris. Lauren had begun working for the care facility that had been her mother's final home. When they first arrived, they'd spent a few weeks sightseeing, and Vivian stated she didn't want to leave. She sold her house and bought a secluded farmhouse on the outskirts of Paris. It was nice and peaceful. They spent many nights on the balcony, watching the sunset with nothing around them except nature. For the first time in a long while, Lauren felt at home. She supposed that's why she had gotten up early. She'd been restless, tossing and turning. She hadn't wanted to disturb Vivian, so she escaped to the living room.

Lauren looked back to Vivian and shrugged. "Just thinking."

"About?"

"About how happy I am. I never thought I'd end up living here, with you."

"Then why do you look so sad?" Vivian reached up and smoothed the lines on Lauren's forehead.

"I'm not sad, just have a few things on my mind." Vivian didn't look convinced. "I promise I'm okay. I just have this weird feeling in my gut like something bad has happened." Lauren shook her head, trying to dispel the disquieting feeling. This was their first Christmas together, and she wanted to make it special. She kissed Vivian. "I was thinking maybe we could go for a walk before breakfast."

Vivian's eyes widened, then she glanced out the window. "Honey, I don't know if you noticed; there is a snowstorm going on. I don't fancy traipsing around in a blizzard."

"Come on, it's not that bad out there. Just a little flurry." Lauren grinned. It'll be fun. We can build a snowman."

"Fine. But promise you'll warm me up when we get back in."

"Always."

Vivian got off Lauren's lap and padded to the open-planned kitchen. She switched on the kettle. Lauren rose, intent on getting dressed. Her mobile rang from the coffee table. She saw Damien's name flash on the screen. *Probably calling to wish us a happy Christmas.*

"Hey, big Bro. Merry Christmas."

"Lauren, I have something to tell you."

Lauren's heart rate picked up at the serious tone of Damien's voice. She blindly sat down on the coffee table behind her. "What is it?"

"It's Dad. He had a heart attack at the office yesterday. No one was there to help him, what with it being Christmas Eve. He was found, last night, by the security guard. Lauren, he's gone."

Lauren blinked. Her mouth seemed unable to find words. She hadn't spoken to Gregory since the night at Damien's, back in April. Gregory had tried to talk to Vivian a few times, even showed up at the house once, right before they left for France. Vivian changed her number, and they hadn't heard from him since. Lauren didn't think he even knew they were out of the country. Damien had kept to his word and hadn't seen him either. She didn't know how to feel now Gregory was dead. She still thought of him as her father.

Despite his deplorable actions over the years, she never wished him ill will. He had left them alone. Lauren was happy, Vivian was happy, and Gregory never much crossed her mind.

"Lauren, you still there?"

"Yes."

"What do we do?"

"I don't know, Damien. I suppose he'll have a will somewhere, with his funeral arrangements."

"I guess I'll go to the house and see if I can find it. Will you come home?"

Lauren looked over her shoulder to the kitchen. Vivian was leaning against the countertop, watching her with a worried expression. Lauren turned away. "I don't know. We weren't on speaking terms. I don't think he'd want me involved in his funeral."

"I wasn't asking for him. I was thinking of you being here for me and the kids."

Lauren sighed. Of course, Damien would want her support. He had always been close to Gregory. Until recently, Damien had no problems with him. "I'll book a flight as soon as I can. I'll let you know when I'm arriving."

"Thank you, Lauren."

Lauren hung up and tossed the phone onto the couch. She stood and went over to Vivian. "I'm not sure how much of that heard."

"Only your side. Gregory?"

"He died yesterday. Guess my gut feeling was right."

"Are you okay?"

Lauren blew out a breath. She felt a little guilty that she wasn't more upset by the news, but she couldn't find it within herself to cry. He was still her dad, but he'd treated her so badly over the years. Her hatred for him overrode any feelings of love.

"I'm fine. A little shocked, but I'm not upset by this. I feel sorry for Damien, though. Does that make me a bad person?"

"Oh, Lauren. Of course not. You have no reason to feel guilty."

"Damien wants me to come back, to help him with arrangements and things."

"I'll let my boss know I'll need a couple of weeks off."

"You don't have to come with me."

"Yes, I do."

Lauren smiled. "Thank you."

"You're welcome." Vivian stepped forward and hugged her. "Come on, let's go see what flights there are. Unless you want to drive?"

"No, it's too far and will take too long. The sooner we get there, the sooner we can get home."

Vivian glanced out the window. "Do you think we'll be able to get the car through the snow?"

"Shouldn't be a problem." Lauren went to the window and peered outside. The snow had started to settle on the hills, but the road leading from their driveway to the main road was clear. She turned back to Vivian. "The road looks fine. If we get a move on, we should be at the airport before it gets any worse."

"Can aeroplanes even fly in the snow?"

"If the runways are clear, then yes. Let's look online and see if the flights are running." They spent the next twenty minutes looking for flights. Lauren's plans for leaving early were put on hold, as they could only get a flight for later that evening. The blizzard was due to stop within the next couple of hours, so no build-up of snow would impair the plane taking off. "I'll call Damien and let him know we should be there by tonight."

"What shall we do for the rest of the day?"

Lauren frowned. Their first Christmas together was ruined. She had wanted to make it special for Vivian. They had planned to open presents and cook a nice lunch together. The afternoon would have found them snuggling on the sofa watching as many Christmas films as they could before retiring to bed. It was a simple plan with no stress. Just the two of them. Lauren's mind wasn't up for that now, and she felt bad for letting Vivian down.

"I'm sorry, Vivian. I'm not going to be in the mood to do what we'd planned."

"Why are you apologising? This isn't your fault. We'll have plenty of other Christmases together."

"I know, but I wanted to make this special."

"Lauren, every day with you is special. Just do what you need to do, and I'll be here when you need me."

At that moment, Lauren's mobile rang. She grabbed it from the couch, seeing her uncle's name flashing. No doubt this would be the first of many calls from friends and relatives of her father. She sighed. "I'd better take this." As she swiped to answer the call, her thoughts turned to all the things she and Damien would need to get sorted. For the next week, minimum, her life wouldn't be her own.

†

Early the next morning, Lauren knocked on her father's front door. Damien answered, looking like he hadn't slept all night. His hair was a mess, and his eyes were ringed with grey. She could just imagine how many phone calls he had received. She herself hadn't got off the phone until she boarded the plane in France.

"Hey, Lauren." Damien smiled sadly and hugged her. "Thanks for coming."

"It's good to see you."

"Come in. I've made coffee. Let's sit in the kitchen, and I'll fill you in on everything."

Lauren followed him into the kitchen, removing her wool coat as she did so. A chill ran through Lauren's body, despite the warm house. It was creepy being there and knowing her father would never step inside again. For years, Gregory had built his home, filling it with possessions and memories. It saddened Lauren that those memories would never be remembered by him, that his belongings would be gone. It hadn't been this hard when her mother died. When Celeste became too ill to stay in her home, Lauren had a few years to work at the task of dispersing her things. The long process had been more manageable. Knowing Gregory's things needed to be sorted sooner rather than later brought an unpleasant feeling to her chest.

"Where's Vivian?" Damien filled two cups with coffee and passed one to Lauren, who added milk to her own.

"I dropped her off at her sister's. She wanted to come with me, but I thought it best if we did this by ourselves." Vivian hadn't been happy about leaving Lauren to tend to the task but acquiesced to her wishes. Lauren took a long swig of her drink. "Did you find his will or anything?"

"Not his will, no, but I did manage to get into his safe. I found instructions for his solicitor. He has Dad's will and is the executor. I called him yesterday afternoon and set up an appointment in two days. I also found information on the funeral directors. They'll make arrangements to collect his body and transfer him to the crematorium." Damien took a shuddering breath and lowered his head, tears forming in the corners of his eyes. "I can't believe he's gone." He looked up at Lauren. "He worked so hard his whole life, gave up on Mum and you. Wasted time he could have spent with his family, his grandkids, all so he could make more money. And for what? He died bitter and alone. I don't want to end up that way."

"Damien, you're nothing like him."

"Are you sure about that? I work eighty-hour weeks, sometimes more. My kids are growing so fast. I'm afraid I'll turn around one day, and they'll be off living with their own kids that I won't have time for."

"The fact that you're standing here worrying about that proves you're not like him. You have the chance to make a change."

"I've been thinking about something. Between sorting through his paperwork and fielding phone calls, I've decided to sell the yacht business."

"What?"

"The health club has been doing well. I want to open the chain, as you had planned, but turn them into a franchise. I could work normal office hours. I wouldn't need to be so heavily involved."

Lauren gazed at him. His mind appeared to be made up. It sounded like a good idea, but she didn't want him to make a snap judgment. He had worked so hard on the yacht business, and she knew it meant a lot to him. "Take some time before rushing into this. Talk to Michelle."

"I will. I just don't want to miss out on the important things in life."

Lauren agreed with him. That was the main thing she'd come to realise while she was in Scotland after Vivian left. Trying to make a name for herself with the health club had been a good idea at the start. Once Vivian was gone, she learned that life without someone to share it was pointless. She didn't want money and prestige; she wanted a family. Lauren reached over and took Damien's hand in her own. "You're right. Having a family is a blessing. One we should feel lucky to have."

Damien smiled and kissed her cheek. "Oh, I found this too." He went over to the opposite counter and retrieved an envelope. He passed it to Lauren. "I found it in the safe. I didn't open it, as it's addressed to you."

Lauren squinted, as she read her name in her father's handwriting. She glanced at Damien. "What do you think it is?"

"No idea. Just open it."

Lauren pursed her lips for a moment, then ran her finger under the flap. She pulled out a single sheet of paper. The mostly blank paper bore only a name and an address. She blinked. *Peter.* Her breath left her in a woosh, as she read the name.

"What is it?"

"It's the name and address of my biological father."

"What?"

Lauren handed him the piece of paper. "Do you think Dad knew where he was all this time?"

"Maybe. Or maybe after you went to France, he felt guilty and tracked him down."

Lauren shook her head. "I'm not sure I like either one of those options."

"What will you do?"

"I have no idea." Lauren was thirty-seven. Was there any point in finding a man who probably had no idea she even existed? *What could I even gain from finding him? It's not like I need him in my life.*

Damien must have sensed her reticence. "We both just agreed that family is what's important. If there's a chance to get to know him, you should take it."

"Maybe." She took the piece of paper back and stuffed it into her jeans pocket. She would talk to Vivian about it later. For now, they had other things to be getting on with. "Did Uncle John talk to you about a gathering for the family?"

For the next couple of hours, they went over the memorial her uncle wanted and began sorting the house. They couldn't remove anything until the will was read, but Damien wanted some kind of order to things. He also wanted to get rid of the perishables in the kitchen. While they worked, Lauren's mind kept coming back to the piece of paper in her pocket. For all she knew, it was an old address. Peter probably didn't even live there anymore. He could have already died. She pushed that thought from her mind. Damien deserved to have all of her focus.

†

Lauren swiped her key card and unlocked the hotel room door. The main light was off, but a small lamp next to the bed illuminated her path. Vivian reclined on the bed, reading. Their eyes met, and Vivian lowered her book. Lauren closed the door and made her way over to the bed. Seeing Vivian looking refreshed and relaxed stirred a kernel of jealousy in her gut. The time was fast approaching ten. Lauren had spent all day at Gregory's, and she was dead on her feet. All she wanted was to curl up next to Vivian and sleep for the next ten hours. She bent at the waist and kissed Vivian on the lips.

"Hello, my love." Vivian reached up and gently feathered Lauren's hair. She shifted over, allowing Lauren room to sit down. "How's Damien?"

"He's okay. Looks tired." Lauren undid her shoelaces, then toed her trainers off. She swung her legs up on the bed and leaned back against the headboard, accepting Vivian's head as she rested it against her shoulder. "I think this has hit him pretty hard. I know he hasn't seen Dad in a few months, but up until that point, they were close." Lauren had always been envious of their relationship, feeling like the outsider she was. Now Gregory was gone for good, she felt bad for Damien. The bond between them had been broken because of her, and that didn't sit well in her heart. *If I hadn't asked Dad for the investment, they would probably still be close.* She couldn't help but wonder if her actions had led to Gregory's heart attack. *Damien still wouldn't know Dad wasn't my real father.* Would they have all been better off continuing as they were? Or was knowing the truth the right thing all along? So many questions Lauren would never get answers to. *I suppose it doesn't matter now.*

"Did you get everything sorted?"

"Mostly. We have a meeting with Dad's solicitor in a couple of days to discuss the will."

"That's pretty quick, isn't it? You haven't even had the funeral yet."

"The paperwork Damien found in Dad's safe said for it to be done as soon as possible."

"What about Bridger Holdings?"

"Damien said Dad's new CFO is handling things for now. I don't know what will happen in the future. A year ago, it all would have been Damien's. After everything that's happened, I'm not sure if Damien is even in the will. I doubt that I am" Not that she minded. She had never wanted anything from Gregory except for his love and support.

Vivian lifted her head and turned toward Lauren. "How are you feeling about it all?"

"Honestly?" Vivian nodded. "I just want to go back home and be with you." The last seven months in France had been ideal. The slower pace of life gave them more time to get to know each other and fall deeper in love. Vivian wasn't stressed over her job, and Lauren loved helping out the residents in the care home. Country life suited them. Although Vivian missed her family, they both wanted to remain in France for as long as possible, maybe forever.

"How are your mum and sister?"

"Everyone is fine." Vivian grinned. "My sister is pregnant again."

"Wow. How many is that now?"

"Four."

"She's braver than me."

Vivian glanced away for a moment. "Have you ever wanted kids?"

"I've never really thought about it. I haven't exactly had any long-term relationships in the past. And then Mum got sick. I was so busy looking after her that a partner and family never really came to mind."

"What about now?"

It was clear her answer would be an important step in their relationship. Lauren didn't want to give the wrong response, so she threw the question back at Vivian. "Do you want kids?"

"I think so. I've always enjoyed spending time with my nieces and nephews. Seeing Dianna so happy about having another... I guess it would be nice to have a family of my own." Vivian looked wistful for a moment, then she grinned. "I'm not exactly getting any younger though."

Vivian was right. If they wanted to have a baby, they would need to start planning soon. They weren't old, but Lauren wanted to be able to run around with the youngster and guide him or her through life for as long as possible. She envisioned what it would be like to hold their baby for the first time. Her thoughts wandered to the first day of school and maybe having grandkids. A warm sensation coated her insides. All her life she had wanted a proper family, but it had mostly been just her and her mum. *Raising a family with Vivian would be amazing.*

"I think I'd like to have a baby. As long as it's with you."

"I suppose that's something we can talk about in the future."

"Yeah." Lauren looked away and stared at the far wall. All the talk of a family brought the piece of paper in her pocket back to mind. She had done a good job of not thinking about it for most of the day, but now it was front and centre.

"Is there something else on your mind?"

Lauren nodded. She stuffed her hand in her pocket and pulled the paper free, clenching her fist around it. "Damien found an envelope in Dad's safe with my name on it." She opened her hand and passed the slip to Vivian. "That's the name of my biological father."

"Oh, wow."

She watched Vivian unfold the paper and gaze at the few words that carried so much weight.

"I don't know how long he had the information. That envelope could have been there for years. I'll never know if he was ever going to give it to me."

Vivian looked back up and rested her hand on Lauren's thigh. "That's got to mess with your head."

"It has." Lauren took back the slip and carefully laid it on the nightstand as if it would break. "I don't think it matters now whether he was keeping it from me all this time. My only concern is whether to track Peter down or not."

"I think you should."

Lauren raised her brows. "Really?"

"I do. Your mother told you about him when she began to get sick. I think she wanted you to know the truth so you could find him one day."

"I'm nearing forty. Do I need to meet someone who has had no meaning in my life for all this time?" Lauren had been shocked to learn the truth, obviously, but she had been focusing on Celeste's illness. Whether he was out there somewhere never crossed her mind. Gregory was her dad. Despite his treatment of her, she never once considered

213

trying to find her biological father. All that changed when she opened the envelope. It was easier when she didn't know his full name and had no idea where he was. Having the piece of paper with his details sparked her interest. She was curious to know what he looked like, what made her mother fall for him, and if he ever knew he had a daughter out there somewhere.

"What does your heart tell you?"

"I think I'd like to try to find him. Even if I only meet him just once. It would be nice to know where I came from. Maybe he can tell me more about how my mother was back then, why she had the affair."

"You could have other brothers or sisters."

"I guess." Lauren closed her eyes, as melancholy sprung up in her chest. "Vivian?"

"Yeah?

"When will my life not be filled with trauma and heartache?"

"Oh, honey. Come here."

Vivian opened her arms, and Lauren turned into her. She wound her arm over Vivian's hips and laid her head against Vivian's chest. She screwed her eyes shut to keep the tears in. She wasn't normally such a vulnerable person. Anger was usually her go-to feeling. After spending the day going through her father's things and boxing stuff up, and now talking about Peter, her emotions came to the surface. She felt safe to allow those thoughts and feelings out in Vivian's presence.

"I'm so sorry for all the things you've gone through and are still going through," Vivian murmured. "I promise, it'll get better."

"Will you always stay by my side? Everything is easier now you're with me."

"I promise." Vivian's kiss to the top of her head was tender. "I love you."

"I love you so much." Lauren lifted her head so she could see Vivian's eyes. "If I had to go through all of this again to find you, I would. Every tear was worth shedding as it brought me closer to you. I never want to be without you."

"And you never will be." Vivian kissed her. "Come on, let's get some sleep."

Lauren untangled herself from Vivian and got off the bed. She stripped herself naked and crawled under the covers, into Vivian's arms again. She wanted a shower but didn't have the energy. The pull of snuggling with Vivian was too much to resist. Vivian leaned over her and switched off the light. In the darkness, they rearranged themselves into a comfortable position. Before Lauren knew it, she was fast asleep, wrapped securely within the safety of Vivian's arms.

CHAPTER EPILOGUE

Vivian glanced at the GPS and rolled the car to a stop. She turned off the engine and gazed at Lauren. "Are you ready?"

"As I'll ever be."

Vivian smiled, when she noticed Lauren's hands shaking. She reached over and stilled them with her own. She scanned the area through her window. At eight in the morning, the park was virtually empty. A couple of dog walkers roamed the perimeter, while a lone man sat on a bench. Vivian squinted her eyes, trying to see if there was any resemblance to Lauren. "I think that's him on the bench over there."

"I'm nervous."

"Don't be." Vivian turned back to Lauren. "You've spoken to him on the phone. He sounded nice."

"What if he doesn't like me? I don't think I could take that rejection again."

"It's a possibility, but it doesn't matter. You owe him nothing, and I'll be here when you finish to give you all the love you need."

Lauren took a breath, then blew it out slowly. "You're right. I no longer have to impress anyone, except you."

"You impress me every day. Go on, before he thinks you're not coming."

"And you'll be waiting here?"

"Right here in the car."

"Okay. I love you."

"I love you. Now go."

"See you soon."

Lauren took another breath and opened the door. Vivian watched her cross the short distance to the man, her gait not her normal, confident stride. Lauren spoke to the man for a second. He stood and hugged Lauren awkwardly, then they set off walking. *That must be him then.* After Gregory's funeral, they'd wasted no time in going back to France. Talk of Peter was scarce, but Vivian knew he was on Lauren's mind. She would catch her staring off into space, sometimes fiddling with the slip of paper that was now crinkled and worn. It had taken two months to finally decide she was ready to try and meet him. After some checking, it turned out the address was Peter's current location. It was clear that Gregory had been keeping tabs on him, at least for a while. Lauren had cried that night, knowing Gregory had kept that from her. The next day, Lauren wrote Peter a letter telling him who she was. She hadn't expected a response, but a week later Peter called. They spoke for an hour and finally agreed to meet.

As Vivian tracked their progress around the field, she thought about the last year and everything that had happened. She was so in love with Lauren. She never thought she'd find someone so right for her. They were even looking into sperm donors. Vivian suggested using Damien's sperm. That way, Lauren would have a genetic link to the baby. Lauren wasn't so keen on the idea at first but was slowly coming around.

The only upset that had caused an argument was after the reading of Gregory's will. Bridger Holdings was bequeathed to Damien, much to all their surprise. However, he vehemently stated he didn't want the responsibility and was in the process of selling the company off. The biggest shock was that Gregory had left his house to Lauren. She hadn't expected to be in the will, so finding out she had a ten-million-pound property had floored her. Like Damien, she refused to accept the inheritance. She wanted nothing to do with a place she had no happy memories of. Lauren tried to sign it over to Damien, but he didn't want it either. He already had his dream home. Vivian had come home one day and caught Lauren researching land developers. She intended to knock down the house and sell the land off as cheaply as she could. Vivian was dumbfounded Lauren could do that. The house had been in the Bridger family for decades. To simply bulldoze all that history was horrifying to Vivian. She could understand Lauren not wanting to live there, but there had to be other options than simply destroying it.

The argument between them hadn't lasted long. Lauren realised her idea was a knee-jerk reaction to the trauma

Gregory had put her through. After talking it over for hours, they decided to gift the property to the local council on the provisory it be used as a community centre. The council was thrilled at the offer. Damien even donated funds so the council wouldn't have to pay out of pocket for renovations. It had been a good decision; one Vivian was proud Lauren had made.

Everything in their lives was perfect. Vivian had no doubt there would be a few bumps along the way, but with Lauren by her side, she knew their future was going to be one filled with love and laughter.

Lost in her thoughts, she didn't notice Lauren approach the car until the passenger door opened. "How did it go?"

"Good. He's pleasant. He asked if we wanted to have dinner tomorrow night before we go back to France. He wants to meet you and wants us to meet his wife."

"That sounds great."

"Yeah." Lauren looked down at her lap, frowning.

"What is it?"

"I feel weird."

"How do you mean?"

"I don't know, like something is missing." Lauren gazed up at Vivian, and her frown turned into a smile. "I don't feel tense or angry. I've felt that way for so long that the absence feels strange. It started to lessen when I met you, but with everything with Dad, the feelings still lingered. I feel free. Finally, free."

Vivian leaned across and kissed her. "I'm so happy for you. I love you."

"And I love you. You have no idea how much you being with me has changed my life for the better."

219

"I do know, because you did the same for me. Now, how about we head back to the hotel? I'm feeling frisky."

"Step on it."

Vivian laughed, as she started the car and headed in the direction they had come. The next forty or more years lay before them. Vivian knew they would be exhilarating.

ABOUT SAMANTHA HICKS

Samantha currently lives in the south west of England with her best buddy, Finley, her springer spaniel. She spends her time writing, drawing, and getting out into nature. Family and friends are the most important things to her, and she finds her inspiration for her stories from those closest to her. Writing has become her greatest passion, and after years of trying to find her confidence, shes finally decided to make a career out of it. She hopes to be doing this for the rest of her life. Sam has a thirst for reading, preferring it to almost anything, and she hopes, one day, to settle down by the beach.

OTHER AFFINITY BOOKS

<u>The Ghost of East Texas</u> by Ali Spooner
Agent Blair Cooper and her partner, psychic Tally Rainwater, (Terminal Event) are back in a gripping new murder mystery investigation.
When the serial killer Casper Caruso, known as The Ghost of East Texas, was sent to death row, Agent Blair Cooper was adamant that there were more victims of his killing spree. As his execution day approaches, Casper reaches out to Blair. If she agrees to a face-to-face meeting, he will give the whereabouts of 10 additional bodies left in his wake.

<u>The Star Child by Ali Spooner</u>
Eli and Whit are enjoying their life together on the mountain when Whit is called into action for a secret mission at the Pentagon. While she is gone, the Cast Iron Farm comes to life, literally, when Eli discovers a mysterious cave that has a

connection to Whit's past. Younger brother Brad joins the gang. When Whit returns, she plans an Appalachian Trail adventure with Brad and Mitch. Join Eli and family as their adventure at Cast Iron Farm continues.

My Dear Vet by JM Dragon
Ava Lawrence, a research veterinarian, is thrown in the deep end when her uncle asks her to cover his country practice while he has a vacation of a lifetime. How could she refuse? His team shouldn't be any different than the crew at her parents' practice, oh, was she so wrong. What she now has to work with is a sassy nurse, an obnoxious receptionist, and an animal whisperer, or so it seems. Ava finds herself embroiled in taking care of animals in the area and local issues outside her experience, making her question her sanity. Throw in chickens, cats, dogs, and a donkey named Theo, along with various other animals. This turns out to be Ava's unexpected adventure with far reaching romantic benefits.

One Shot at Love by Annette Mori
Blair returns to her hometown after the death of her sister. Always an activist she vows to use her voice to advocate for better gun control. She meets Maribel, an irresistible, sexy woman who proves to be an enigma to Blair. Maribel can't help approaching the weeping woman and learning the origin of Blair's grief, Maribel thinks she is the last person who should form a friendship with Blair. Ultimately, the allure is too much for Maribel, but how long can she keep her secret and continue to nurture their burgeoning feelings for one another. A committed left-wing social activist could never

fall for the poster child of the NRA. Unless taking that one
shot at love matters more than anything else.

The Mountain Whispers by Ali Spooner
Arriving home and discovering the betrayal by her best
friend and lover, Eli Fortner leaves to run off her anger and
hurt. A chance stop at a convenience store and the purchase
of lottery tickets sends Eli's life into a whirlwind of change.
Able to now pursue her dreams, Eli heads off to see what
else fate has in store for her.
Whit Brewer, Eli's neighbor, is everything Eli never knew
she needed and wanted. But can she let go of the betrayal
long enough to let Whit in? Thirteen black cats, a baby goat,
and Cruz, her furry best friend, join Eli on her adventure,
new life, and the possibility of real love.

Charlie by Erin O'Reilly
At fourteen, Hannah Garvin met 'the one,' Charlene Gaines,
and her life was never the same. They were inseparable and
spent every moment they could together. One day, Charlie
left without a word and again, Hannah's life took a dramatic
change. Hannah vowed to never fall in love again. When she
meets Mick, a new arrival to the small Texas panhandle town
near her family's farm, her heart remembers what being in
love was like, and yearns for more. Will Hannah let the
memory of Charlie go so she can start a new life with Mick?
Or will her heart betray her and hold on to her love for
Charlie?

Misha's Promise by Renee MacKenzie

The Boss's Daughter

Misha Wyatt has settled into a peaceful existence as a healer in Karst, New America. When an airplane crashes in the meadow outside of Karst, Misha hurries to help the pilot. Misha is not expecting the pilot to be alive...or so beautiful. Will her uncontrollable desire to keep the pilot safe be her downfall? Can *they* survive their journey? The last book in the Karst series brings our characters to their physical and emotional limits. Don't miss the culmination of this exciting series!

Heart Strings Attached by Ali Spooner & Annette Mori
Socialite Remy has her world shaken. Bartender Chancy has her orderly life turned around. A mutually beneficial business agreement between Remy and Chancy turns into undeniable attraction. Will the two ignore culture norms to explore their intense desire for each other?

The Panty Thief by Annette Mori
Someone is stealing panties, but who? And why? Joey Hartford is a fourth-year medical student who insists she doesn't have time for a relationship. A new tenant in her apartment building is proving too tempting to ignore. Sabrina is in her final year of her doctoral program and focused on completing her dissertation. Meeting Joey is dangerous for so many reasons. Add a suicidal ex-girlfriend who suddenly reappears in Sabrina's life and Joey's jealous friend-with-benefits, and things get complicated quickly.

Country Living by Jen Silver
Peri Sanderson achieves her dream of moving from London to a cottage in the English countryside with her wife, Karla.

Peri sees their future as pastoral while chatting with the locals in a quaint village pub. Sexy urbanite, Karla, has other ideas. Secrets are everywhere. Peri quickly senses something not quite right among her rural neighbours and also with Karla. Temptation, betrayal, and intrigue combine to change the lives of both women beyond anything they could have imagined.

Before the Light by Samantha Hicks
One year after her long-time partner Meredith's abduction and their subsequent break-up, Kathleen Bowden-Scott's life is spiralling out of control. She meets Bethany Jones and despite an instant attraction Kathleen shies away. In this fast-paced, romantic suspense, lies are exposed and hearts unite as Kathleen and Beth fight for their future.

Affinity
Rainbow Publications

eBooks, Print, Free eBooks

Visit our website for more publications available online.

www.affinityrainbowpublications.com

Published by Affinity Rainbow Publications
A Division of Affinity eBook Press NZ LTD
Canterbury, New Zealand

Registered Company 2517228